When Clouds
Take Form

WARREN ARMOUR

DEDICATION

To my Mother and Father, and the ancestors I never knew.

CONTENTS

ACKNOWLEDGMENTS

This book would not have been possible without the support of family and the willingness to open a rich oral tradition. I give great gratitude to Editor Anita Bunkley for her professional assistance.

CHAPTER 1

Our tall lanky two-family flat was planted in the most vulnerable of positions, right on the lively corner of Bacon Street and Montgomery Street in North St. Louis. Lucky for me, or as much luck as a seven-year-old boy needed, we occupied the second floor, towering well above the battlefield of our Jeff Vander Lou neighborhood. The earthy base of the yard surrounding the home was nearly five feet high, fortified by dirty white cobblestones around the outer shell, facing the streets and the alley. The position of the windows left no blind spots, creating a perfect theater for gangbangers, drug dealers, and addicts below.

Mother seemed to be a world away, remaining in her front bedroom, distracted by the only television in the house. My younger twin sisters, Kya and Keisha, with whom I shared the back room, were entertained by clapping games or whatever piqued the interest of five-year-old little girls. No matter what they did, it was so synchronized you'd think they practiced being twins at times. I usually had no interest in the duo's games, as my collection of army men, lined along the windowsill at perfect strike position, was all the entertainment I needed.

Just yesterday, while stationed at my observation post, looking out the window to Montgomery Street, I spotted Stink and a troop of four walking toward the nearby liquor store. For almost anyone else, this trek wouldn't have raised the hairs on one's forearms, as it did to me that day. But Stink was a reputable gangbanger from Slattery Street, a few blocks east of our house. He was an almond-hued, brown-skinned frail kid with spider twisted hair, who was confined to a wheelchair due to consequences of past bullet wars, I presumed. The gang's main rivals were the Bacon Mob, who happened to have family members living at the house directly across the street from mine. The intersection of the crews would most likely have only one outcome, a stained street, and the soulless glare of stuffed animals bound to a utility pole in memoriam.

Major drug connections, seeded years ago in the mid 80's from far away South Central L.A., were now linked with the already seasoned thugs of Midwestern St. Louis. This painted our gangs with identifiable colors, where no palm tree would ever last the winter. I knew the Slattery gang simply as any neighbor, as I had played football on the vacant lots with little brothers of the Bacon Mob. And here marched Stink, flanked on both sides of his war chariot, and guarded by two to the rear, all clad in cherry red. I never quite understood why the members announced their presence by wearing their gang colors loudly conspicuously, and Bacon Mob was no better, with group allegiance airbrushed on t-shirts and mesh snapback caps. I watched as Stink and his troupe inched towards the Grand Avenue liquor store with the skittishness of white tailed deer in an open field, hands not too far from their waists, ready for any inkling of

2

trouble. I ran to the other window facing Bacon Street, eager not to miss a clash ensue on the tip of our lawn, but the backs of the gang slowly faded into small red dots under the trees.

For a second, I thought about the false sense of power I held over these young black males, walking under my snotty nose, from the window up high. A simple shout of "Eeeeewhooopp" would have alerted rivals to spill out of their front doors, right into the lap of instant bloodshed. This distinct vocal command, which sounded more like an animal mating call than any secret speech, was a coded language I had observed the gangs using while initiating drug deals at a distance, or used as an alert of danger. I humored myself many days, shouting it out the window and ducking, while the Bacon Mob's heads would swivel in all directions, confused by this foreign interference. I would laugh and laugh, holding my mouth as if they could hear my giggles. Mother caught me one day and warned me to stop unless I wanted to get my head blown off. This day I did not wish to incite violence, and probably more of what mother had said on my twisted amusement stuck with me.

This was the climate of the JVL area in the early 1990's, concealed explosions patiently waiting to detonate at the slightest pressure or misstep.

"Quinn . . . boy, I know you hear that," mother shouted from up front, in reaction to the sound of metal banging on kitchen pipes. We didn't have a phone on the second floor of our walk-up flat, and any time Mother got a phone call, Granddaddy Sharp, would bang a hammer on the open pipes downstairs to let us know. The arduous annoyance of having to go outside and walk all the way downstairs just for a simple phone call. I slipped into Mother's dingy, once-white house shoes as I dredged my way towards the back door.

Mother hissed, "If you don't put on some fucking shoes."

I sighed, but did as instructed and giggled under my breath as I often did at Mother's cursing; she was the most creative of cussers, and the twins and I couldn't help but laugh even when she was mad. I also knew she didn't allow me to go out of the house without a shirt on, or wearing proper shoes. No matter that the other boys in the neighborhood could play outside shirtless, especially during the St. Louis unforgiving summer days, but Mother insisted going shirtless was a sign of no home training, and didn't allow it in the least.

Opening the screen door, I was jabbed with the foulest smell, stopping me in my tracks. The scent of a rotten vermin pushed me back inside, closing the screen door. "That smell?" I screeched and crumpled my face, clearly offended by the odor.

Mother's eyebrows raised and stiffened as she gave final warnings to put pep in my step. I knew any further hesitation would lead to a butt whooping, so I moved on. I headed down the mountain of steps facing the alley, with the foul smell of death lingering in a pestering mist. I spotted one of Granddaddy's aluminum pie pans that he put out in the yard to feed stray alley cats, and immediately made up my mind about the odor: One of his ragged cats must've become victim to a mean old dog. I could picture the culprit, chiseled, eager, and primed for the act. That had to be it, I thought. It had to have happened in the schoolyard, the two critters circling one another in a standoff on the black pavement, snarling and growling the whole time. The ragged cat, maybe the fat white one, rushed in a valiant effort, landed three quick strikes, but was no match for the jaws of the brindle beast. He'd be remembered for his courage. Poor cat.

My teenage cousin Ashley lived downstairs, along with my Great-Grandmamma Flo, and Granddaddy Sharp who was actually my Step Great-Grandfather. They were my Mother's dad's parents, sharecroppers from down in Arkansas who still had some of that country left in them. You could catch Granddaddy gutting a reeking largemouth bass right there in the backyard, or grabbing that old' shotgun and loading up the station wagon to go rabbit hunting on the weekends. He had an underground bunker that cut right into the five feet of earth surrounding our house, with a narrow walk space and dirt mounds on either side that acted as shelves for tools. A secret dungeon, if you asked me.

Grandmamma Flo greeted me at the door in a long blue housecoat to give me the phone message. I hoped she had baked a pound cake today, or maybe a pie. I loved to escape the limited options of fried spam and saltine crackers we usually got upstairs, plus it was my only chance to watch cable television. I'd hop in Granddaddy's recliner chair and become entranced with the Nickelodeon shows like Salute Your Shorts, Hey Dude, and Wild & Crazy Kids. Those Nickelodeon kids were kooky and comical, and surely happy as hell, but nothing captured my fancy more than when Timmy & Lassie came on. A boy, no bigger than me roaming open pastures with his loyal companion, fighting wolves, saving old ladies, and running off outlaws. It was a dream: if only I'd had my very own Lassie, there certainly wasn't a shortage of crimes we'd get to clean up right here on Bacon & Montgomery.

Today, I didn't make it to the recliner. Usually I'd charm my way in, and the only real cost was sometimes having to recite Yes, Jesus Loves Me as Grandmamma Flo had taught the twins and me. However, after the phone message I was sent on another errand by her to deliver mail to Baby Brother. I did as told, feeling mildly disappointed that I had to continue to fight this foul mist. Baby Brother, whom I called Uncle Bo, was the youngest son of my Great Grandparents. He stayed a block away in a rundown shed on a small triangle island of land surrounded by Garrison Avenue, Coleman Street, and Montgomery Street at its base. I didn't really understand why a grown man would want to live in a beat up old garage. I figured it had to do with the whispers I'd heard that he wasn't quite right in the head anymore, people said the Vietnam War must have really messed him up. Before I could even make it to Coleman Street, I heard Uncle Bo's piano. He was playing a melody and shouting his jazzy shoo-boo-do bops to the heavens. He also had a wide piano tucked in a corner of my bedroom back home that he'd come up and mess around on sometimes. I guess he got more of a kick out of performing right here on the streets. I slowly pulled back the already cracked wooden door on the sagging shed, allowing the sun to shine in, revealing his jerry-curled head swaying about like Stevie Wonder. He gave me a nod and smirk to acknowledge my presence but never stopped his Doo Wops, and kept right along playing. I leaned comfortably against the splintered wood and made an audience for his one-man band.

In the gleam of the sun, I spotted a figure approaching, just as yellow as the sun itself: spaghetti stick legs became visible in the shade and I recognized it was Crackhead Rose. She walked with excited purpose and her big head bobbled about on her wiry frame. "Where yo momma at?" she greeted me, sucking her teeth after the sentence.

After a brief exchange, she asked me to remind Mother to stop by her house later. I took her presence as my cue to leave Uncle Bo's concert and stay out of grown folks' business. The putrid smell had only slightly faded as I made my way back home. I paused at the alleyway entrance and wondered about its real source. Like most happenings in the neighborhood, I was left to figure things out without much adult explanation. I would have to learn that navigating was just as important, if not more important than discovery.

CHAPTER 2

Mother fumbled her right hand around in a plastic bin of barrettes at her side, searching for whites and purples, her left hand holding a twist on Kya's head as she sat between her legs on the floor. Mother used her mouth as third tool, holding black rubber bands between her middle teeth, an open-face gold tooth with a star design twinkling at the top. Included with the distinct permanent gold, she had a natural, black, beauty mark centered between her nose and lip, highlighting a pretty round face of even, dark chocolate skin. Being such a young and vibrant Black woman at only twenty-seven years old, it was an oddity to most that we addressed her as "Mother." How she explained it one day years ago as we were getting on her last damn nerve, saying, "Momma this, momma that, can I have some of these momma. Where we going momma?" She was at her wits' end, and instructed us, "Don't momma me ... not a nudder damn, hell time." She continued, "Call me Kasmira."

The first name basis only lasted about a day before she settled on Mother, and it had stuck ever since. How funny it would have been to call her Kasmira, I thought. The brief embarrassment and chiding we got from other kids due to having to say "Mother" was expected. We tried saving face by using "momma" in the streets, but over time, we no longer really cared. Mother was "Mother."

The twins' hair was finally done identically. They put on matching colorful outfits and powder white canvas tennis shoes that we called white girls. Even though the twins were fraternal, most people couldn't tell them apart, so they just lazily called them Light Twin and Dark Twin. Kya and I shared Mother's smooth dark complexion, but Keisha was the sole one with a honey caramel complexion.

Mother, the twins, and I headed towards the convenience market on foot, as we usually did, and I hated it. What could have lasted thirty minutes, turned into hours, most times. Mother was a beautifully friendly spirit, and she would talk and talk and talk until the next stop. Everyone knew her … from old church ladies to street youth whom she'd greet, "Wassup lil derrty," as I would bury my face in my hand in embarrassment at her acting hip. I'd feel the same bashfulness when she threw her deceased father's name around (Duke Brock) to random OGs, asking if they knew him from back in the day. Apparently, he was a man of fear and respect, as sometimes we got free stuff, but suffered even longer conversations mostly. After a few talkative pit stops, we finally made it to the convenience market over on Glasgow Avenue, where Mother ripped off a couple of single one-dollar bill food stamps for me to use as I liked.

I thought momentarily about the temptations of making the brown paper stamps stretch as long as the aisles, and I certainly had a gift for doing so. I pocketed one dollar and the other went towards 2 Chick-O-Sticks, 1 green pack of Now & Laters, 1 box of Lemonheads, 1 box of Boston Baked Beans, 4 Crybaby pieces, and the rest in mixed Frooties. I then stuffed my face in an *Inside Wrestling* magazine at the newsstand while Mother talked and talked to some stranger. I wished many times I could take the magazines home but Mother would never buy a dumb wrestling book. I finished reading three magazines by the time she was ready to go, so it all evened out.

We made our way to Rose's house on Bacon Street, which was actually her dad's, the Bread Man. He was an old man who drove a dirty van with sliding doors on the side: it was filled with loaves of different types of bread and pastries he sold around town. I knew he took a fancy to my mother because he gave us free loaves, but I never wanted any of that crusty old bread. I wasn't upset at his chivalrous acts; I was used to men hollering at Mother, she was indeed attractive. They'd shout out, asking her name, to which she'd reply something silly like Black or Sally, and keep walking with her chin turned up with a smirk. I'd dry puke at the goofy flirtations. The Bread Man had a gaggle of white and grey geese honking about in his front yard, and it was wonder to me, having such weird pets. And I was more curious as to why they never flew away?

Inside, the Bread Man kept us kids company while Rose and Mother disappeared to the back. For the short time we were there, I stood observing the huge fish tank in the living room filled with swampy water. It was green and muddy and no creature should have had to live in those harsh conditions. I could barely make out any fish, but every now and then the ugly face of a long catfish, much too big for the tank, would peek through the muck.

As night fell, the house was silent, all but for

Mother's pacing feet going back and forth from her bedroom closet while she was searching for what was missing. I sat on the middle end of her bed, arms stiffened at my side, gazing at her every frantic move. She was in a quiet panic, trying not to wake the twins while checking under every crevice, searching and searching. I couldn't help her. I couldn't help, not because I wasn't a caring son, but because I'd hoped she'd never find what she was looking for. I prayed she'd never be this disheveled, empty, and lost again. The truth was, I knew Crack had her, and here he was pulling her body about by strings, with jerky and unnatural movements.

I was too young to remember when it first started, but it was too heavy not to recognize it on my Mother, and it weighed down on me, on this house, only the thick ground kept us up. She didn't wear it on her body like the crackheads in the streets. On our walks I could see their bugged eyes, rotten teeth, loose jaws, frail bodies, jittery movements, pale skin, dirty clothes, distressed demeanor, soullessness, and desperateness. There were no missed meals in our house, no missed days of school for her children, and no missing items being exchanged for a quick fix. She smiled and joked, talked and talked, and had a nature as bright as the gold on her tooth. But she was an addict, a fiend, a dopehead.

From her panicked trance, she escaped for a second to recognize I was there, watching her every move. She paused, and stared at me directly with squinted questioning eyes.

"I threw it out the window," I said to her, very matter-of-factly and with a sternness that I would have got popped in the mouth for under different circumstances for talking smart. I had studied her routine and knew she hid the small silver pipes used for smoking crack in between a wooden panel in her bedroom closet. When her attention was diverted earlier in the day, I grabbed what I could reach and tossed it out the window. I hoped I could throw the pain of the addiction out into the street, and wished it never to return.

"Boy, are you crazy?" Mother asked, frustrated. She turned towards the next room but continued talking, "Now, what if Granddaddy finds that out there?"

I didn't answer, I just watched her continue searching with a closed left fist tightly gripping a lighter. She found her drugs, and made her way back to the closet, the flicker of the lighter now the only sound in the house. She paused and tilted her head back with a deep exhale, letting the drugs take effect. Mother turned to me, still stiffened on the bed, and attempted to talk, "Don't you . . . for Granddaddy. . .what if. . ." She paused as the drugs continued to sap at her soul. Whenever the crack would take its debilitating effect, her thoughts were incomplete and she couldn't manage full sentences. She was high now, and I had failed to stop it.

The next morning, Mother came to me somberly and sobered from last night to address the addiction that she knew I already knew she had. "You know what month it is?" she asked.

I shook my head, confirming I didn't understand, even though I knew it was August, but I couldn't piece together what the month had to do with last night.

"You know, it a really tough month for me, August 20th is the day my momma and daddy died. Not died, killed," she corrected herself and muttered, "I hate when people say died." Then she continued, "They were killed, five years apart on the same exact day in August. I was the same age as you when my momma got killed. I'll never forget: Me and your TT Darcy were outside playing, and your Grandmamma White called me over to the porch said, 'Your momma's gone baby, she's dead.' I looked at her right in the face, and asked, Can I go finish playing?"

"You didn't even cry?" I interjected in disbelief at what I was hearing

"Na uh, I went back out and finished playing, but no, I didn't cry. I think I may have when my daddy died five years later, just a little bit though. After twenty years, I still haven't had a real cry, but it's been with me the whole time, it's never went anywhere. But I feel it, especially in August, it's there. And the drugs...I don't know...I just know they have a large part to do with losing my parents like that."

There was a lot more to the story, I suspected, but I chose not to press her on that morning. What for me was the month of a nearing new school year, and the summer's last chance to bully you into submission in the humid hell of the St. Louis heat, was an unkind reminder of death and a snatching of childhood for my mother. Innocence taken in blood, now being confronted by numbing of the spirit through drug use. Her heart was hardened and her eyes were long deserted of tears. Though I thought I understood, I still couldn't help but feel hopeless. Mother had sparingly touched on her childhood before. She described her momma Dorothy as having brains and beauty, with the perfect body to boot, but the only problem was Dorothy knew it. There was a bit of a sophisticated arrogance about her: she had goals and didn't mind telling anyone to get out the way.

Duke was the source of mother's pride, with smooth dark skin just like hers, and the same confidence. A real playboy. The cold truth was he was a no nonsense gangster and an unapologetic cutthroat, and whether they were headed to the deli or church, he kept his folded newspaper at all times concealing a black revolver. I knew Mother and TT Darcy were raised by my Great-Grandmamma White, who now lived a short walk up the block on St. Louis Avenue. They would be overindulged with affection, as the daughters of Dorothy and Duke, their parents both deceased. Grandmamma White would raise them as best she could, and with padded love from the many aunts and uncles for the poor little lost girls.

CHAPTER 3

By good fortune, my feet caught up to Mother's shoe size over the summer, as I had to wear her navy blue *Ellesse* sneakers on the first day of my second grade year. It was the best I could do; my freshness was not in the least bit a factor of importance, and she didn't have any extra money for new kicks anyway.

While walking to Columbia Elementary, where I attended, my only focus at the moment was hoping Uncle Bo wasn't in his shed singing his Doo Wops. I just couldn't start the year off with that embarrassment in front of friends. I took a sigh of relief seeing the shed was silent. As I made it to the blacktop unscathed, I was greeted by my best friend Charles by the schoolyard gate. "Wassup Homie?" he shouted, wearing a cheesy grin on his face. "I got something for you," he said while reaching in his pocket, pulling out a sterling silver money clip in the shape of a dollar sign.

"Oh snap, let me see that shit."

"Yo, you can have it, I don't even want it."

"For real?"

"Yep."

Now, I don't even want it meant one of two things; it was either a stolen item that you needed to get rid of or you had something even better of your own. I gladly accepted the gift without question, as it was pretty much law, knowing the only two options meant not to pry any further. The silver money clip was just a small token in our bigger dreams of grandeur, like on field trips when we would playing Keylock on the school bus. The game consisted of shouting "keylock" at flashy cars on the highway that we wished to have, to claim it before the next person could.

We had a monopoly on the pretty girls as well; we'd hand them a ballot on notebook paper and ask them to name all the boys they liked in class. We won in a landslide every time, I'll admit, due to a little gerrymandering, as our names were the only ones on the ballot. I guess they could have written someone in if they really wanted to.

While walking to other areas from our classrooms, and into dimly lit hallways was where we enjoyed our spoils, pinching butts of girls who snickered bashfully but always found their way in front of us. Money, cars, and women, none of which we needed in grade school, and certainly didn't have, as we were dirt poor. The reality of being poverty-stricken surely didn't subdue our illusions; in fact, it made them stronger and kept us afloat from drowning in our sorrows.

My diplomatic ways kept me in good graces with most students and teachers alike. Although, Mother deserves most of the credit, she didn't tolerate any acting up and I never missed school. I could code switch in the snap of a finger from the blacktop with the homies to dealing with eager teachers in the classroom. It made it easier that I was always one of the smartest kids in the class and the teachers mushed over me being so well mannered, although it got uncomfortably embarrassing at times.

There were a couple kids who weren't so lucky and always got the shit end of the stick. First, there was James, who was the only white kid in the school, and probably the only one on the entire Northside of St. Louis, for all I knew. I peeled him off the floor a few times; he was like a once-battered stray dog who jumped at the slightest of hand movements. I don't know why his momma put him through that hell every day?

Then there was Dexter, a beanie head boy who wore the same pissy corduroy pants every day. He was a master thief who could steal the eraser right off the pencil in your hand. One morning last school year, I saw him on the little kids play area surrounded by eight kindergarteners swinging away like Evander Holyfield. Dexter looked like Goliath among the pint-sized kids, but they kept coming and coming at him. I admit, the little kids were annoying, but it made absolutely no sense to pick a fight with them. I thought I'd exercise my diplomatic ways to see what the hell this was about and break it up before teachers arrived. I slowly walked toward the fracas. I could hear Dexter huffing and puffing while throwing hooks but no words came out; the little ones were still nipping at his heels.

I got close enough to jump right smack in the middle but thought better of it. I reached out and tapped Dexter on his back left shoulder. He pirouetted like an Olympic ice skater at lighting speed. I could see a big brown fist angling towards my face with his elbow tilted towards the sky; then wham. His fist crashed flush on my jaw, snapping the lower half of my face away from the fight, and the upper part of my face looking back over his head. My body stumbled back three steps and I caught balance enough to solely concentrate on the pain I had never felt before. I glanced back to see the fighting had stopped as the hook shot to the unintended target of my face had frozen everyone.

I turned back towards the big kid's playground with watery tears now flowing down my cheeks. I held my lower jaw tightly in place to keep it from falling off. I was greeted by Charles and a couple homies who inquired about what had occurred. I was in too much pain to talk, but apparently they pieced together what happened and charged towards Dexter, who didn't wait around to see what they intended to do to him.

We all made our way back to Ms. Young's class, who was an older black woman who was always stern and quick to put a child in his or her place. Before class could start normally she stood up and called out to me in front of everyone, "Quinn, would you like to explain what went on outside?"

I slid my hand away from soothing my face and wondered how she knew what had happened. I hesitated and said, "Oh … oh, I'm alright."

"I didn't ask if you were alright, now both of y'all get up here." Ms. Young was more upset than her normal angsty self, and obviously knew there was more to the story before trying to put me on the spot.

She centered Dexter and me squarely in front of the whole class, face to face like two world champs before a title match.

"We not gon have nun of this. Now he hit you right? Gone hit him back just like he hit you," Ms. Young instructed. She folded her arms and waited for the order to be followed. I turned to Dexter, processing my next move and really wishing I had not been put in such an awkward position. He faced me directly but I could tell his eyes were going right through me; his anger was boiling and increasing by the second, his face was tight and the only sign he was breathing was his shoulders slightly inching up and down. I looked over his body, wondering where to hit to get it over with, as a punch to the face didn't feel proper in this setting. I focused in on his fleshy stomach poking out from under his snug sweatshirt. I pulled back and threw a hard straight right to his belly, hoping he'd crouch over in agony like the wrestlers did on television. He didn't budge; it was like punching a tree. I could feel whatever pain or anger he harbored shielding his body in solid armor. I anxiously looked back at Mrs. Young for assurance.

"Is that how he hit you?" she asked.

"No" I nervously answered, conceding that the pain I felt outside couldn't have evened out with the body shot he just ate.

"Well, do it again."

I pulled back and fired another shot to the gut with the same force. Dexter's face didn't change as he absorbed this punch even better than before. Ms. Young shooed me away to my seat seemingly frustrated, and grabbed a wooden paddle from behind her desk. I didn't pay attention to how many times he got whacked with the wooden paddle. I was fixed on his face waiting for any sound to come out that never came.

CHAPTER 4

On Fridays, with Mother's permission, we'd walk down St. Louis Avenue after school and spend time over at Great-Grandmamma White's house for the weekend. She lived just a few houses down in a walk-up apartment in a four-family flat with only her oldest son, my Great-Uncle Dan. She greeted us at the door in her long white silky housecoat and her favorite wig. The only time I saw her in anything different was on Sundays, wearing her white gloves and big gaudy hats while waiting for the church bus. But most of the time, she sat at the end of her bed in her housecoat watching her stories, The Young & the Restless and Guiding Light.

Uncle Dan stumbled in, smelling like beer and outside, to the dissatisfaction of Grandmamma White as she gave him an earful about what needed to be tended to around the house. He found a corner of the wall end, and rubbed his back, finding the perfect scratch like a grizzly on a redwood tree. "I - I - Imma get to it, woman," he stuttered in between groans of satisfaction from being scratched. I laughed at the exchange just I'd always done, knowing full well Dan would get around to it, but at his pace. He had his own set of rules, for instance, one included only taking a bath on Sundays. I'm not sure it had anything to do with godliness as he never went to church, but by all accounts of smell, he sure stuck by it. I asked Mother once why'd he stay living with his momma all these years when his younger siblings all left, and she stumblingly explained that he was a little slow in the head. But I figured he was just playing a cunning dirty trick, because he seemed just fine to me.

Come early morning, Dan would have us out running store errands for Grandmamma White. He'd drag the twins in a red toy wagon with me tagging along. By noon, I was entertained on the front porch by a collection of Dan's old drinking buddies participating in overly-serious games of checkers. In between my uncle's screams of "next!" as opponents failed in succession, the majority of the competitiveness was vulgar chiding and freaky tales that I knew I shouldn't be hearing. No one took Dan's drunken rants seriously, even though you could sparingly find a gem.

There was one time during our many early morning fishing trips to nearby Fairground Park that his liquor-smelling words made me think. Dan grunted in disdain to my question: I asked him if he knew my grandfather Duke, after asking what his sister Dorothy was like. I could tell that, even after so many years had gone by, he still felt a considerable loss for his sister and had a heavy disdain for her husband on whom he placed responsibility for her death. I quickly changed the subject to lighter topics.

I'd excitedly anticipate staying up late Saturdays nights to catch wrestling and fall asleep on The Three Stooges reruns. Dan somehow would make himself comfortable, resting his head on a steel toolbox on the floor beside the bed. By the time Grandmamma White was putting on her white gloves and waiting to hear the horn of the Sunday church bus, and Dan was running his hot water for his much needed soak, I had time to sit back and miss Mother. I hoped Grandmamma White would say a prayer for her at church that day, even though she was the strongest and most confident person I knew, it made no difference.

The chorus of gunshots and police sirens would tap at Grandmamma's window all weekend, and I wondered why Mother would flirt with the uncertainty of what the nights held. The burden of being just a child, knowing my Mother could be five houses down the street, getting a fix, all while her own Grandmamma didn't know, weighed heavy on my small body. When Mother would finally come to pick us up on Sunday, it all went away, there was a sense of relief that I worried too much: Mother was too strong to let anything bad happen. I disappointed myself for ever doubting her. The diversion of a new Monday always saved me from myself more than I knew.

CHAPTER 5

In elementary school, elevation to the next grade up represents the height of achievement in maturity. For Charles and I, there was no better way to cement our ascension in stature than by getting girlfriends. My courtship, which consisted of publicly acknowledging I liked a certain girl and offering her tokens of Sundance corn chips and penny candy, landed me Shadonica. She was a thin, pretty brown-skinned girl with hair pulled back in a small tight ponytail. Her goofiness was endearing and sweet, and she stood out like daisies in a field. I, on the other hand, was reserved and observant, displaying wittiness over silliness.

The other integral part of going to the next grade was getting a new teacher. With Ms. Young's foot finally off our necks, there was room for a breath of fresh air. I could tell Ms. Young had had a fondness for me but I was glad to have a new teacher in Ms. Calloway, who wasn't so militant. Ms. Calloway was a fluffy–haired, middle-aged woman with a sweet and gentle approach that could make a boy feel sorry for himself if he ever acted up.

Today, Ms. Calloway pushed out the television cart for a showing of Beauty and the Beast, as a reward for some good behavior milestone. The class huddled around the television, sitting Indian style, and every which way, on the cool, white-tiled floor. Charles and I inched into position at the sides of our girlfriends, only half-heartedly interested in the dancing and singing teapots and candlesticks in the movie.

Shadonica leaned in receptively, the gentle friction of our arms slightly touching warming my body. . I felt at ease, my arms now propped on my raised knees, as I watched the cheerful characters sing their hearts out and dance about. My eyes were fixated on the screen when I felt Shadonica lean in with warm puckered lips and kiss me on the right cheek. There were a few teasing groans and snickers from the few that saw, made softly so Ms. Calloway wouldn't notice.

I raised a slight smirk at the onlookers, only a little embarrassed but feeling cheerful inside for my first kiss. I truly had the upper hand on Charles now, neither of us could have seen a kiss coming. I had to be the luckiest boy at Columbia Elementary. I sat still while emotions slowly swirled in my core, then suddenly I couldn't concentrate on the lively characters in the film, but I could hear their songs. I lowered my head between my knees and stared downward. I felt a tear follow the curves of my nose and splash onto the white floor. I watched as the drops quickly became a puddle.

"He's crying," someone whispered softly.

Shadonica bent down to get a better look at my face. "What's wrong?" she asked. "Did I make you cry?"

I sniveled, trying to suck up tears, and quickly shook my head to affirm she wasn't at fault for anything.

"Then what's wrong?"

I paused to try to gather my thoughts, but that only made me confused. I didn't know what the source of my sorrow was at the moment. I felt alone.

"Ms. Calloway, Quinn's crying."

The teacher gently lifted me by the armpit and led me to the hallway. "Did they do anything to you? Are you hurt? Was it the movie?"

A deep sadness constrained my face and didn't allow me to speak. I could only shake my head, expressing no to all her questions.

"Do you want your mom? Come on, let's go call your mom."

I sat in the principal's office with dried tears on my face, worried about what Mother would think. I never got in trouble and I never missed school. I knew once she walked down those steep stairs from the banging of Granddaddy Sharp's kitchen pipes, she'd come accompanied with a leather belt. I was upset for ruining my moment with Shadonica, and missing a perfectly good movie day, too. Mother arrived in no time and I could hear Ms. Calloway struggling to explain what had happened. After the talking stopped, Mother led me out on Garrison Street towards the house.

"Quinn, now what the hell is wrong with you? Don't you know them white folks will take you away from me….. in there crying like that? You wanna be separated from your sisters?"

"You - I mean I, I was thinking about you...you using drugs," I said, finding my voice again and feeling a small sense of relief getting out those words. I still wondered if I had been thinking about Mother all along, and why words couldn't come out of my mouth in the school.

Mother sighed deeply and looked away, into the wind. "Yeah, I figured that what it was. I'm trying . . .I'm trying. You know I've been working on something, and we're about to get the hell up out of this neighborhood for one. We got a new house, and we'll be moving soon. And y'all got approved to go to school out in Clayton, so you tell that Ms. Calloway you won't be back next year."

I couldn't believe how exhilarated I felt about the news. My eyes now dry and cleared, all my sadness seemed to be left back on the school floor, and I hoped the move would push me farther away from it. I had no idea what a Clayton was, and even though I'd miss Shadonica, Charles, and the rest of the guys, I still couldn't wait to deliver the news. I glanced at Mother to see she was still staring in the wind, the excitement I held wasn't shared by her at all.

I thought about the time she told me about Grandmamma White, when she had to come down to the school like Mother just did for me. How she didn't have the young pretty Mother that was hip and could talk the talk like we did in the schoolyard, and how she would hide to avoid kids asking why her momma was so old? The tight wigs and lipstick were not able to hide the years traveled or forgotten, revealed in wrinkled lines on her face. Mother told Grandmamma once to never come to her school again because she was so hurt by the shame of it all. And even worse was the teasing from some cruel kid who knew about her parents being dead. All the fights would follow for simple respect and peace of mind. Unlike me today in class, she never cried out either ... not once. I couldn't help but think about what Uncle Dan said about my Grandparents. Could some Shakespearean-like tragedy really have played out? Star-crossed lovers spilling blood in the streets of St. Louis, leaving a cursed little girl unable to cry? I couldn't bring myself to ask Mother; we could only just walk and wonder with the truth buried deep under our feet.

CHAPTER 6

Mother had not always been lost in a tattered wind, but whatever there was to preserve from a virtuous childhood would take exemplary will to keep hold of. Her warnings to her little sister Darcy didn't mean anything now; she knew what would happen next would be bad. Very bad. At only the age of four, Darcy didn't yet understand the skill of lying for a greater good. "Well, he asked, and I told him the truth," Darcy pleaded to Kasmira, fighting back tears of disappointment and confusion.

"Shush, be quiet I'm trying to hear what's going on." Their father, Duke Brock had already run downstairs, chasing after Dean Ruffin, the new boyfriend of his estranged wife Dorothy. Duke had just asked the girls, "Has that nigga ever laid a hand on you?" While Duke certainly loved and protected his children with every fiber of his being, his daughter, Kasmira, knew his underlying motive was really about the separation from their momma, Dorothy. Rolling high in exploits of the heroin drug game, from his luxurious raven black Lincoln Mark 3 to the tailor-made satin suits and dark shades, came a trail of women that he indulged in, one after another. Kasmira and Darcy would have a few half-brothers and sisters spread about St. Louis due to Duke's extramarital affairs.

Dorothy grew tired of it. She was a beautiful young woman at only 26 years of age, and she looked to shape her own path of happiness. Dorothy made it clear she was moving on and started a relationship with Dean Ruffin. Kasmira could faintly hear the screaming and barking from Grandmamma White's window as her parents quarreled outside. Then thunder erupted. Had it not been for the sweltering sun of August, the girls would've thought it was a rainstorm, but the sound was gunfire flaring out front.

Duke pulled out the pistol he was known to keep tucked in a rolled newspaper and taken everywhere he went, and fired at Dean as people scattered and ducked behind cars. Dean Ruffin returned fire, sending bullets piercing into Duke, which gave him time to hop in the car with Dorothy and speed off to safety. As blood poured, Duke hurried to the nearby Negro hospital, Homer G. Phillips, for treatment on his bulleted body.

The next few days seemed like an eternity for Kasmira and Darcy, even after hearing the calming news that their father's injuries were not life threatening. At seven and four years of age, they still had to juggle the weight of feeling responsible for the bloodshed that had just transpired. Only Grandmamma's prayers and soothing love could provide a brief break from the turmoil.

A week later, while Duke sat in the hospital recovering from his gunshot wounds, in another location Dean Ruffin pulled up to the City Methadone clinic for treatment, with Dorothy in the car. The clinic was a hotspot for dealers and addicts alike; heroin flooded the streets of St. Louis, and like most patients, Dean had a set routine for treatment. As he exited the building and sat in his car out front, bullets immediately poured into the vehicle from a vacant building across the street, tearing through hard glass and metal into soft unsuspecting flesh. The wounded passengers were rushed off to Homer G. Phillips Hospital with Dorothy clinging to life.

In only a week's time, Grandmamma White would again have the ill-fated task of explaining the brutal wickedness of adults to the children.

At Homer G. Phillips Hospital, Dean Ruffin was much too restless and high-strung to be concerned about Dorothy's condition or his own bullet wounds. He knew shooting Duke Brock a week ago was a confirmed death wish, and that he was the intended target in front of the clinic and only had God to thank for his life being spared. Now he didn't know if Duke was still at the same hospital or not, as every door sliding and drawer closing was felt like impending death. He made a long-distance call to family back in Chicago, within hours, armed guards and a private ambulance from Cook County arrived in St. Louis. An Illinois State Policeman escorted him back safely to Chicago, never to be heard from again.

Four days later, on August 20, 1973, Grandmamma White returned home from the hospital wearing profound sadness on her face. She called out to Kasmira, who was playing around with some neighborhood kids, "Baby, I just came back from the hospital, okay … your momma - your momma didn't make it. She passed away. She died, baby," Grandmamma White said with cheeks twitching rapidly, unable to dam the flow of tears.

Kasmira looked back with blank childish eyes, giving a nothingness. "Can I go finish playing now?"

she asked, to which Grandmamma White could only nod in approval.

Duke would recover, and never took a break from his lifestyle as a gangster; not even the murder of his young wife could change that. It was all he knew. His ruthless reputation was cemented, even as the walls of the infamous Pruitt-Igoe housing project where his crew made their name was torn down in an admittance that the government's housing complex was a failed death trap. Old gangsters with whom Duke ran, like Terry Cooley and TJ Ruffin were dead. "Fats" Woods and Earl "Killer" Williams were facing federal drug indictments, but Duke still pushed on with younger gangsters on the rise like Jerry Lewis and the Petty Brothers.

As Kasmira and Darcy grew older, they would slowly learn the unpleasant truth of their father's lifestyle and the people he ran with, but their love never waned. Darcy would be glued to the hip of Grandmamma White for the most part, but Kasmira was a daddy's girl. Duke would spoil them with treats, take them on fishing trips, and catch Cardinals games at the old Busch Stadium. It was a little bit of normalcy after the tragic death of their momma Dorothy White, who was so loved and missed dearly by her family.

But the gloomy and perilous underworld would eventually catch up to Duke. On August 20, 1978, exactly five years to the day that Dorothy died, Duke Brock was found dead with a bullet to the head. The St. Louis Evening Whirl newspaper would say on its front page, THEY FINALLY GOT HIM. Lightning in the form of brutal murder struck twice on the same day for Kasmira in the span of five short years, leaving her with no parents and a cursed hot August 20th anniversary day.

CHAPTER 7

Amazingly, it took two bombs before we could move in our new pale yellow duplex at 4957 Lotus Avenue. The roaches must have been indestructible on this side of town, and I still choked on the foggy air from the pesticide can we let off, which lingered in the atmosphere for over a week. Our modest home went mostly unnoticed in the neighborhood of gingerbread houses, where sweet gum trees lined the sidewalks and spiked balls crunched under each step, driveways were paved in black asphalt, and stone lions stood guard in front lawns. It was a far cry from the seedy streets of JVL.

My obsession for my own Lassie never really subsided, and now that we had a fenced backyard and a basement, it was the only thing in the world I wanted. Since I knew Mother would never buy a dog, I decided I had to take matters into my own hands and scour the neighborhood for a needy stray looking for a home, like they did in all the movies.

I recruited Kya and Keisha to be my assistants on the dog hunt. We packed a gym bag with old belts for leashes and snuck some of Mother's ground breakfast sausage to use as a lure. We would walk and walk all the alleys along Euclid all the way past Highland Avenue and Maffitt Avenue. We would always come up empty, envious of the Channel 4 news lady's family behind us with their annoying Miniature Schnauzer, and the police lady a couple houses down with her beefy Rottweilers. We pressed on with little luck.

Our fortunes changed one afternoon without even packing for a hunt when I looked out our oval topped living room window and saw a small ball of scraggly white fur and patches of brown. It was a pup no more than four months old, with a wolfish nose and pointy ears that stood erect as he sniffed around the yard.

I stumbled off the couch, yelling for Kya and Keisha to come on; there was no way I could miss this opportunity after so many failed hunts. I didn't have time to grab any food. I picked up a blue nylon belt and jetted out the front door. I inched closer and closer while the little dog seemed not to care much that we were there. He ignored my puppy-talk and was more curious with the scents around him. I realized that we had never really been prepared for the prospect of actually bringing a dog home on our trips. Here was one right on our lawn, and it didn't give a damn about my presence. I eased in, determined to win its favor, and was able to get close enough to pet his hindquarters, only a minor victory in my pursuit. Feeling confident, I looped the holed end of the belt inside the buckle and pulled, making a makeshift leash and collar. The twins looked on nervously as I slowly slid the belt loop over the sharp-muzzled nose and onto its neck. "We got him," I screeched, keeping a tight grip on the tip of the nylon belt. All the miles walked surveying dirty alleys and looking behind dumpsters had finally paid off.

I let the pup take lead around the yard unknowing he'd been captured to be our new pet. We gingerly made our way to the side of the house and I just had a few more feet to get him secured in the backyard. My fingers stretched toward the fence latch and the tension of the belt tightened for the first time. The pup jerked away, offended by the stress of the nylon, jumping back on two legs. He shook every which way, like a wild horse, as I struggled to reach the backyard. He quickly gave up pulling and turned his attention towards my shins, rushing in, showing teeth. I extended my arm to create distance while still gripping the belt, avoiding the snarling snaps of this little white and brown monster. I saw the twins standing, wide eyed, at a safe distance, and thought to myself, "I can't hold on for much longer." I threw the belt down and jumped away, narrowly escaping a bite and made a dash for the front door. The twins needed no instructions as they took off as well. I had never been so relieved to be inside the house. It was clear I would have to retire our dog hunting expeditions and think of a new approach.

CHAPTER 8

Learning the new school bus pickup stops and times took a little bit of an adjustment. Columbia Elementary was only a stone's throw away from our house, after all, but now we were being bussed out to the St. Louis County suburb of Clayton, Missouri to attend school. For Mother, this might as well have been another planet; she never traveled anywhere and knew only her familiar stomping grounds of St. Louis City. Even family members moving out to the County became too far for a visit, but the City ... she knew like the back of her hand.

I was humbly given a lesson on proper etiquette of my new neighborhood before the bus even arrived. Waiting at the bus stop one morning at Euclid & Cote Brilliante Avenue, a young light-complexioned black male no older than 21 approached me, seemingly out of nowhere. He lifted my turned baseball cap and shifted it to the opposite direction and pulled it snug on my head, then he continued on, walking away without uttering a single word. I stood there perplexed, not knowing until much later he could have been saving my life at the time. It was a reminder that gangbanging culture had swarmed every corner of St. Louis City, and you'd be forced to shift your attire, depending on the avenue.

Crossing over Delmar Boulevard into Clayton quickly faded the rosy perception of the houses back on Lotus Avenue. These homes in Clayton were scaled-down castles with old-fashioned mailboxes and American flags as the only reminder that an actual family and not some haughty Queen lived there. The school bus dropped black kids off at Captain Elementary, Meramec Elementary, and finally Glenridge Elementary where we attended school in the district. Just like the homes, the school was enormous, with a playground so long that you couldn't see the end of it, and there was a sea of white children, more than I'd ever seen in my life, with different shades of blonde and brown loose hair that flailed as they ran.

I took notice of a large amount of them on the smooth blacktop, intensely kicking a gold ball around in a competitive game of soccer. Many of them dressed the part in small *Umbro* shorts and high socks; I could tell this was the preferred game of choice. Oddities like tetherball and four square were contenders for second favorite, I would learn. There were no familiar games of 21, no spoon break, no joaning contest, and no double dutch for the girls. We were cast into a new world, bearing the realities of our homes and carrying our own customs as studiously as we did our backpacks. For the first few months there would be an inquisitive dance amongst the students, a clumsy curiosity of each other's cultures, and the learning of the steps to how each got where we stand here today.

There was the time a white kid named Joel who had dyed blonde hair chopped off at the sides like a Good Guys doll, tried to engage me in class.

"So where are you from?" he asked.

"...I'm from St. Louis."

"No, I mean, like where are you from?"

I was confused into silence. Was there more meaning to this question, did he think that the African in African Americans meant a specific country in the Motherland? I wondered. "You know, like Brentwood, Richmond Heights, or Manchester ... ? he added, trying to provide understanding. He rattled off a bunch of places Mother would consider far far-away lands.

"I don't know...I'm just from St. Louis," I answered, still a bit befuddled. My teacher, Ms. Smith, a sweet young white woman who also had to add translator and liaison to her tireless teaching duties, jumped in to save the conversation.

"That's right Joel. It's just St. Louis. Now you guys run along to your stations," she insisted, turning a delicate ruby red in the face. My only conclusion was that he thought St. Louis City just hosted Cardinals baseball games or something, but people didn't actually dare to live near there. Another time, a kid named Adam, who had a pure but goofy apprehension about himself, asked, "Quinn, why do Black kids say 'finna'? I'm 'finna' go to the bathroom. I'm 'finna' go to lunch."

Again I was stumped. Ms. Smith, who must have had an extra ear for shamefully awkward moments, jumped in stating, "Finna means Fixing to." I had never heard anyone say "fixing to" a day in my life, but I trusted she was right. I had a few of my own queries about them as well, but I mainly wondered why their moms packed string cheese in their lunch boxes? What a mystifying snack, I thought, all mushy and pale white, but I never had the courage to ask them. The two worlds were a mixed salad much more so than a melting pot of come togetherness. There was mostly peaceful curiosity that never really turned into any level of true culture clash.

On our busses leaving the ghetto we'd harmonize SWV lyrics in-between roast sessions, and then would be playing Hot Cross Buns from sheet music by noon. Our tribal nature only activated in true unison at lunchtime, creating the unofficial "black tables," but all were welcome to a seat at the table and many came, creating new friendships. I had no earthly idea that I was part of any citywide desegregation program or a byproduct of St. Louis' ugly and long history of redlining. I was no longer "the man" like I was with Charles back at Columbia Elementary, and I wasn't the smartest kid in the room anymore, but I still felt good. I may have been just another minority on a piece of paper on some crabby guy's desk, but I knew I deserved to walk those fancy halls and search the excessively huge library just as any other kid.

CHAPTER 9

The Mississippi Delta roots showed out in Grandmamma White's house all year. The hambones smothered in white beans, thick buttery grits and white sugar, fried catfish and meaty spaghetti, all made Thanksgiving a tad less fancy. Stuffing our massive family into this little flat on St. Louis Avenue was the enjoyable part. It was the only time I saw Grandmamma White's sisters, who all strangely had milky vanilla-hued skin. They surely would've passed for white women out in the streets. TT Darcy arrived in town in full military gear from her base in Georgia. Cousins and cousins by the droves were there, and Cousin Larry accounted for half of them by himself. Last count we took a few years back was at sixteen children. For Dan, it meant he met his ultimate match in verbal tussling with his younger brother Elmer. Uncle Elmer was the second oldest of eight children behind Dan, and had moved up North to Detroit many years back.

"Say wh - wh - what do you know little brother?" Elmer chidingly asked Dan with the same stutter that all of Grandmamma's kids had.

"I'm the big brother and don't you forget it," replied Dan sternly, not in the mood for the irksome games.

"Oh yeah, then wh - why are you still at home with

mommy?"

"I'll leave mommy's house when you have a kid, still shooting blanks out there, huh?" Dan countered, causing Elmer to nearly fall over in laughter after successfully angering his oblivious older brother. Gleeful about his minor victory, Uncle Elmer turned his attention towards me, "Say Quinn, here's fifty cents, go buy you a pop."

"A pop? What's a pop?" I measuredly asked, not only confused at the word but also unsure if I was now being fooled in his childish games. You couldn't decipher his intentions by just looking at him; he was as tall as a professional basketball player with midnight black skin and he kept a poker face that held a glass eye. The stories of how he truly lost the eye changed every year, from accidents on navy ships to bar fights. He also told nonsensical stories about how he beat up Muhammad Ali as a Golden Glove amateur, and how he was pals with the singer Donny Hathaway back in his Vashon High School days. Some of it was real, but only he and God above knew the truth in any given moment.

"You know … a sodie pop."

"You mean a soda," I said laughingly as I pocketed the change from his huge fist.

"So-da," he chuckled, adding, "I've been up North too long."

Outside, the wintry cool air wasn't enough to stop a pick-up basketball game that I joined. Our makeshift hoop was on metal railings where a storefront awning canopy used to be, a few doors down from where Tommy Tucker's Clothing store sat on Grand & St. Louis Avenue. Traffic was only a mere five feet to our rear, and there was foot traffic all along the sidewalks, going in and out of stores. I remember once I chased a loose ball to the edge of the curb, and as I kneeled to pick it up, I saw a bulky green wad of money slightly hidden against the concrete. Damon, a chubby kid visiting his family next door to Grandmamma White, ran over as I screeched, unable to hide my excitement. "Ohhh, lemme see. What is that? How much is it? All that money" Damon blurted, pestering me with questions.

"Thirty - forty - forty five dollars!" I excitedly ran to Grandmamma White's shouting back, "I'll see you later." I went right to the bathroom and counted the money over and over again. I couldn't believe it. It was the most money I'd ever seen, so I immediately realized that if I should tell anyone, the adults would surely take it. Before I could make up my mind, I heard a knock at the front door, followed by grownups talking. I took a peek downstairs and could see Damon's round head poking out from behind his momma. I ran back to the bathroom and closed the door, as I just knew it was about the money I'd found. Mother came up, calling out to me, forcing me to come out of my hiding spot.

"What's this about some money you got?"

"I found it in the street in front of the store."

"Damon's momma talking about she just lost forty-five dollars."

"She's a liar!" I moaned angrily, to which Mother immediately gave me a hard correcting glare.

"I mean, she's telling stories ... we were playing basketball, and I found it. Damon musta ran in and told his momma. With her crackhead self," I said disgustedly.

"Boy you better watch yo damn mouth. That's an adult, okay?" Mother said, to which I nodded in agreement. She added, "And that's your money, don't give it to nobody, I knew she was full of shit," turning and walking back downstairs. I smiled in triumph, glad that Mother believed me instead of the shady lady next door. I couldn't understand what kind of person would lie and try to take money right out of a kid's hand. I didn't care to hear the adult conversation that followed. I had supreme confidence that Mother would not only handle it, but would toss Damon's mom over the fence if it came to it. I never played with Damon again.

The aluminum pans got lighter and the trashcan inside the house started to overflow. Uncle Elmer caught me in passing and took the chance to start his jesting. "I hear you out here paying these woman, boy. You giving yo lil girlfriend money?" I knew Mother must have mentioned Shadonica from back at Columbia Elementary, not knowing she was feeding Elmer the ammo needed to turn on me.

"It was just a food stamp," I said, trying to deflect whatever mocking intentions he had.

"A food stamp?" he questioned loudly, unable to stop his burst of laughter. He took the opportunity to bring up further embarrassment. "You remember that time you got lost leaving Fairground?" He was making reference to when I played football for Matthew Dickey's Boy Club, who held practice at Fairground Park on Grand Avenue & Natural Bridge Road. Mother walked me from practice back to Grandmamma's house the first few times so I could learn the route, which was an easy left on Natural Bridge Road, followed by a right on Grand Avenue.

After practice on the first day, when I was walking back alone, everything seemed extremely overwhelming for some reason. The street signs looked taller, the cars seemed faster, and fewer people were out than usual. I stood at the edge of the street with the directions from Mother in my brain all muddled, and blanked my thoughts long enough for my body to turn right and start walking. I walked and walked, but nothing really looked familiar. I convinced myself to keep walking until something was recognizable. Then I noticed the houses getting wide, tall, some shaped liked barns, then wide again but nothing looked like I had seen it before. The black football cleats I wore were barely visible as night fell, and as it got darker, the white pants and yellow jersey of my football uniform got brighter. By the time I passed Taylor Avenue I was in tears. I knew I was lost and didn't have the wherewithal to simply turn around and try going the other way. Everything was so massive, and all I wanted was to see my family one last time before I died. I tearily stumbled upon a stranger using the payphone and asked if he could make a call for me. Mother had made me recite the address and phone number at our house on Bacon Street since I was 4 years old. I was never so happy to see that old station wagon of Granddaddy Sharp's pull up with Mother inside. She was so relieved that I was okay, that she didn't have time to be upset, and I was ever so thankful for it.

Uncle Elmer paused from his chuckling to say, "You know that happen to me too. I was a little bit older than you, and got lost, some white boys pulled up in a pickup truck and start chasing me. They liked to had killed me if I wasn't so fast and got away."

I studied his dark face and could tell for the first time all day that Elmer wasn't being humorous.

CHAPTER 10

My football experience was the first time that I truly felt the absence of my father. Carrying his namesake as a junior, and with everyone calling me "Lil Quinn," his aura lingered with me every waking day. But in the weird mix of youth sports coaches and dads is where an actual presence could have paid off. Before signing up to play for the Matthew Dickey's Bulldogs, my sports grooming came from playing basketball on busted out milk crates for hoops in the alley, and friendly football games always turning into an unnecessary game of Kill A Man; where whoever caught the ball ran suicide into the waiting arms of angry tacklers itching to knock your head off. So it was understandable that it took me a tedious three hours to put on my Bulldog gear for the first time, as I'd never seen a jockstrap or a mouthpiece. I had no idea what each individual position did or what they were called, and the Coach knew too, so I was thrown in with the offensive linemen and pretty much told to just watch the ball and move when it did.

But what I didn't know in technicalities of the gridiron, I had to make up for in pure physical skills. Initially feeling out everyone, who seemed to already know each other, I took a mental note that Chris McMillan and Jeffrey Barnes were the most gifted and most popular on the team. The coaches draped them in praise and never blew hot yelling air in their faces like the rest of the team had to endure. Chris was the star quarterback with confidence and poise like a grown man, and seeing him struggle to squeeze his helmet over his enormous head may have been tangible proof of ego. And I'd heard of Jeffrey Barnes long before I met him; his named floated around in sports circles about him being the fastest kid in all of St. Louis. He walked with a determined focus and didn't speak much at all, but when that whistle blew, he got little in a hurry, bulleting out of vanish point.

Outside of my lower abdomen burning like the inside of a pressure cooker from what were called six-inch drills, we also lined up like thoroughbred horses and raced in an open field. No confusing formations or routes to remember, just good old fashioned "on your marks." This was my opportunity to shine, and I took full advantage. From the first whistle, I planted eager feet in the dirt and shot past everyone with ease, including the myth Jeffrey Barnes.

"Y'all gone let this linemen beat you?" the Head Coach yelled, seemingly frustrated and perhaps puzzled that some pudgy amateur was beating his prized players. He lined us up over and over, thinking the result may be different, but speed came natural to me and I came in first every time. We eventually made it through the harshly humid practices and celebrated everyone making the team at a weigh-in ceremony under strict weight limit guidelines. The only suspense was a heavyset kid named Demario, who was taking laxatives all the way up until he had to touch the scales, and made the cut by half a pound.

It was surreal to see Mother at the first game, looking over the fence in the stands. She was always in her element but now looked hilariously awkward among the fulltime football moms. The stage felt so big as we warmed up and went through the pregame ceremonies. I couldn't believe it was finally here, and I'd play in actual game. I felt a swirl of nervousness and excitement all over my body.

After the initial kickoff, I grabbed my helmet and started to trot out with the offense before a coach grabbed my arm and told me to hold back, while the rest of the guys went out to start the game. All the goofy cadences and routes we had practiced all these weeks at Fairground were being acted out in front of me in our shiny new yellow uniforms. This was the real thing. I figured coach would have me watch the speed of the game before throwing me right into the fire, as it was my first year after all. But plays and plays went by, offensive to defensive possession changed but Coach still didn't call my name. It eventually became clear that I wasn't going to go in that day, and my bewilderment quickly turned to dismay. It didn't help that the guys would come back to the bench asking why I wasn't in there, even an assistant coach asked me if I was healthy and wondered why I wasn't playing.

I was relegated to the bench, and I sat there, lonely, with a jug of lemon juice, taking a few sips out of boredom to pass the time of a game that seemed it'd never end. I couldn't bear to turn around and look at Mother; it was too embarrassing, and she had come all the way out just to see me dangle my feet. Why would the Coach do this to me, I thought. I was the fastest person on the whole damn team. Sure, I was new, but I had learned the position, was always at practice, and never caused any problems. "What the hell did he have against me?" I was left to wonder.

At a timeout, one of my teammates I'd never really spoken to before came over to me and said he overheard Coach saying he was going to redshirt me.

"What's a redshirt mean?"

"Well, it's when you have to sit out, and you don't play unless somebody gets hurt," the boy explained before running back out at the sound of screeching whistles. I glared off towards the short green grass and saw images of the long hot practices, all the coaches standing around talking with fathers about football this and that. I heard the yells of parents behind me but still didn't dare look back. I became angry and lonelier. Why wasn't my father exchanging fake laughs and man-talk after practice like those of my teammates? I didn't have a strong voice that could brag about how his son was an interior lineman and still the fastest kid in all St. Louis. Nobody would believe me if I said Jeffrey Barnes wasn't the future

Olympian everyone thought he was, and I was even better. It had to be that I had no voice, I thought.

I had become more skilled in a few weeks than kids that had been playing for years. "Demario was a snack away from not even making weight, and I couldn't play?" It hurt, and my father was nowhere around to speak up for me.

Mother and Big Quinn were high school sweethearts at Soldan High School. Without Grandmamma White's blessings, Mother snuck out, and she and my father shacked up, soon giving birth to me at just 19 years old. With the sudden unexpected birth of the twins, the young couple had a family of three children by 23 years of age. The mounting bills and mouths to feed became heavy for the two, who wanted to prematurely jump into adulthood. The financial stress led to more arguments, and graduated to fighting. Mother couldn't remember the first time Big Quinn used his fist, then it became so frequent she couldn't forget the last time. What he displayed in uncontrolled rage, only further numbed Mother's soul into an emotionless pit. She often stated she could see even way back at Soldan that his love for her would lead him astray from whatever future he might've had. How her existence alone could sway the comrade of a star football player and school band drummer. The abuse didn't come as a surprise to her; she convinced herself that she brought some of it on.

Ironically, the mind games Mother toyed with and began to act on via infidelity, was never an actual catalyst for abuse from Big Quinn. If he actually knew of any unfaithfulness, only the Lord could have protected her at that point. They would part ways, with Mother and the three kids left to resettle on the top floor on Bacon Street, while Big Quinn's anger led him there only once that I remember, and that ended with Granddaddy Sharp pointing a shotgun to his chest and Mother's brother heaving a brick to his head, putting him in a sudden coma. The wounds on both sides healed, and our trips to our father's side of the family kept on, but his presence became more and more rare.

Before the game ended, I knew I would never put on kneepads for that asshole of a Head Coach ever again. Who would've thought that Kill-A-Man was the epicenter of fairness, and organized football was a crock of shit. After the game, Mother couldn't help but see I was down, but for some reason she was excitedly all smiles. She hugged me and told me how proud she was. I countered, "I didn't even get to play, though." But she just smiled and said, "I know." Her enthusiasm didn't change my feelings; I still never wanted to see Matthew Dickey's again.

CHAPTER 11

By the time the next school year rolled around, being
bussed out to Clayton didn't seem so taxing. We had
cable by then, and MTV videos were our morning
backdrop to brushing our teeth and getting dressed.
For some reason, the same videos played at the exact
same time every morning, and we knew by the end of
Bone's "1st of tha Month" and halfway through
Alanis Morsette's "Ironic," we'd have to be walking
out the front door in order to not miss the bus.
Though the routine of going to an esteemed and
highly ranked school felt normal now, it also was a
concrete reminder of what we didn't have, outside of
a quality education. From the free-lunch tickets we
had to use for meals every day to the *Gamepro*
magazines I'd steal out of the library and circle the
Sega games I wish I could one day have. Even worse
was the fact that I had to start the school year off in
my football cleats; they were the newest shoes I had
and I didn't get a chance to get them dirty after all. I
thought it was a good idea until I stepped off the bus

and my shame grew with each click-clack of the spikes on the blacktop. Matters only grew worse as the entire soccer team on the field spotted me walking an extra inch off the ground and bombarded me with questions as to why I had on cleats. My 'cleanest shoe I had' idea crashed immediately, and my pathetic excuse of planning to play football at recess that I quickly thought of surprisingly worked, but I didn't dare put those cleats on another day.

Mother worked mightily but could only cover so much, raising the three of us alone. She made me call my father for what I needed but I was always reluctant for the fear of being let down. I'd rather go without than add on the possibility of bitter disappointment.

There was the time before I got my Sega when I had been pestering him for a gaming system … as If I couldn't function without it, to which he dropped a dusty old Atari and a bunch of funny looking game cartridges. There was no telling where this thing was from, and I seriously wondered if it was his as a kid. Granted, I did have to play years-old, previously-owned Sega games; lowering the volume and happily playing damn near till sunrise, but they certainly beat an ancient Atari.

Before school this day, I nearly raked my eyes out watching Mother pack me a lunch for a field trip. She piled up two wheat bread sandwiches with lunchmeat and cheese and pickles, grabbed a whole sleeve of honey graham crackers, yogurt, chips, and whatever else she saw that could find a spot in the brown paper bag. I wasn't used to taking my own lunch, but something about this paper bag nearly busting open from the sides didn't seem right. There was an option on the permission slip to purchase lunch at McDonalds, but I knew that the jacked up prices wouldn't fly for Mother and convenience didn't play a factor in my cumbersome life. Furthermore, I didn't understand how a Mark Twain Riverboat had a McDonalds anyway, fast food right there on the Mississippi River … who would have thunk it? The nauseous feeling I felt in my stomach couldn't have been seasickness, because it started while "Ironic" was still blaring from our little television that morning. As the boat rocked up and down under the waves of the vast intoxicating muddy water, I dreadfully thought about pulling out the brown paper monstrosity as lunch neared closer. And there it was, a bright red top and golden arches floating right there near the shore. Quite a few of my classmates fumbled around in their pockets for money, and excitedly began talking about the different ice creams and burgers they'd soon get.

I had my choice of open tables as mostly everyone else was waiting in line, and lunged my bagged lunch up pulling out the immensely thick sandwich first. I wondered if Mother thought we were going on a camping trip; I'm not sure how she expected me to eat all of this food. The smells of desserts, fish sandwiches, and cheeseburgers all kind of fused together and made it easier to ignore those who chomped about around me.

"Yoooo, Quinn what is that?" my classmate Brian asked, eyeing my lunch bag from the next table. I shrugged my shoulders, not wanting to bring any added attention or embarrassment to myself as if Brian wasn't loud enough already. He took my silence as an invitation to walk over and inspect my picnic for himself. "Man, you got all stuff," he gleefully exclaimed, adding "Yo momma packed all of this?"

I nodded, trying not to appear as awkward as I felt inside, as more people made their way over, having already devoured their bought value meals. They began talking, "Uh, can I have this? I want some. Me too. You guys need to share," all pouring from every which way in an unanticipated instance. I nodded approvingly with a glaze of bewilderment in my eyes as my jaws stuck on a bite of sandwich. I didn't understand what was going on, but I felt a weird sense of pride in my mother; maybe she knew more about lunches than I thought.

CHAPTER 12

The sound of popcorn pinging inside the hot pot on the stove came right through our closed bedroom door, which did little to muffle the sound. I tried to hurry through my game level because I knew that popcorn meant Mother would be calling us into her room for movie night. Every weekend, if we didn't get together to watch The Awakening, a low-budget Christian mini-series about inner-city Chicago, then we'd for sure catch whatever the 7 p.m. Sunday night movie was. We'd spread out across Mother's queen size bed: a welcome relief from our cramped bunk bed, and cozy up from the cold that tapped the windows outside.

"Is he dead for real?" Keisha asked for the umpteenth time, watching a guy on T.V. roll around in fake blood while squealing.

"Shut … Be quiet," I snapped, catching myself from saying one of the many non-curse words that Mother treated as actual curse words.

"Yeah, he's dead."

"Quinn, after the show I need you to grab all your clothes together," Mother interrupted in a dull tone devoid of any reaction to our bickering.

"Where we going?"

"I'm getting some help . . . I'm checking into a rehab. It's a place you go to get help from using drugs," she explained. "I got the girl's stuff together already, Gran Gran will be here in a little while to pick us up. Now you know I've always kept y'all together, but you may have to stay with Gran Gran for a little bit, you understand?"

"How long?"

"I don't know . . . until I get better."

I stared into Mother's dark face, her unblinking eyes looked exhausted, like they had been cried out and just needed rest in order to cry again. It felt like I should have been happy that Mother was getting some help but I couldn't feel much of anything. I knew the lady Stephanie that we called Gran Gran; she wasn't our real grandmother or actually related to us at all. Mother said Stephanie dated her father, Duke Brock, back in the day and had loved him to death, just like everybody did. Like most people who loved Duke, after he died they showed their love to his oldest daughter. I remember Stephanie coming around every once in a while and being friendly, but I never expected to have to live with her.

Grandmamma Flo, Nannie (our father's mother), and Grandmamma White had all passed away in the last three years, back to back to back. We had been to so many funerals that anytime anyone died we expected death to come back in threes again. I guessed since we had no Grandmamma left, the next closest thing was Gran Gran.

She arrived at the door wearing a long, dark, wool coat, with a scarf wrapped around her neck and head. Her pale yellow skin beamed out through the dark layers of her tall and slender frame. We left, heading towards a rehabilitation center called Queen of Peace, a treatment center that housed single mothers and offered substance prevention services. The ride there seemed abnormally dark, like we were the only ones on the streets, and it was quiet for the most part, until we felt the long rough cobblestone road rattling the truck leading up to the building. We crossed through a high locked gate and pulled up to a huge ancient cathedral. It was a castle of a building, like something I'd only seen in a King Arthur film. After Mother signed some papers, we were served a funny tasting dinner of a hunk of beef smothered in gravy, mashed potatoes, and carrots in a cafeteria. Mother and I were separated from the twins and were led to an office with a middle-aged white women who pestered Mother with questions. The counselor lady turned her attention towards me and said, "Do you know why you all are here?"

I looked up at Mother, seated next to me in a chair in front of the lady's desk.

"It's okay, you can speak," Mother said assuredly.

"Yes," I replied, staring down into the wood grain of the office furniture.

"And why is that?" the lady asked.

"So Mother can get help and stop using drugs."

"And how does that make you feel when she does?"

I looked up at Mother again, to which she gave a nod of approval to continue. I could feel the tears gradually start to well up in my eyes, and my eyelids trembled doing their best to hold back the flood. Mother could sense my hesitations; here we were in this grand-looking castle in the dark of night, and I didn't know if any word I spoke was the right or wrong thing to say. I just didn't want to get Mother in trouble.

"Bad."

"It makes you feel bad," the lady said, repeating my answer and concluding my short interview.

CHAPTER 13

God I hated cats. Their slow-moving steps and mysterious disposition made them untrustworthy, and unlike dogs, you never really knew where they stood. I finally got some decent sleep for the first time in a week after shutting and locking the door to the bedroom Gran Gran had prepared for me. How was I ever going to get some sleep with a cat walking around? I thought. I could hear Gran Gran calling for me in the distance, "Come down for breakfast honey." I slowly stepped out of the bedroom, hoping not to be encountered by her sleek brown feline. He wasn't in the hallway, but I'm sure he was watching me, from somewhere.

I saw Gran Gran's bedroom door was open and couldn't miss the chance to take a peek. There was another bending hallway inside the door leading to the actual room which seemed a bit excessive, like everything in this huge old house. Downstairs there was a long old-fashioned dining table, chandeliers hanging from mile-high ceilings, and crystal and metal trinkets lined atop fancy-looking shelves. It didn't make sense that this old woman lived here all by herself with all this extravagant junk around. The hall led me to a huge bed wrapped in silky-looking covers: it was high off the ground and I definitely would need a ladder just to hop in. Across from the bed was a drawer dresser with countless jewelry boxes stacked on top. I could only imagine all the fancy pearls and diamonds that were in there. I made my way to the closet and was met by an assortment of fur coats in grays, whites, blacks and a bunch of colors and combinations. Flipping through the luxurious warm coats, a dark chocolatey brown creature dropped at my feet, nearly causing me to lose my stomach right there on the floor. I picked up the weasel-looking furry creature and was surprised to see it had just about all its parts except its thin silky body. It had a head, eyes, mouth, and little feet with nails. "Is this what they wore back-in-the-day?" I muttered. I immediately had a grand idea that this little fake mink or whatever it was would be perfect for our dog hunts, "I could surely leer a dog home with this thing," I said. I stuffed the mink in my shorts and turned to head towards my temporary bedroom, when I saw that deceitful little cat; he must have been watching me this whole time. I sidestepped out of Gran Gran's bedroom, not taking my eyes off the cat until it was safe.

"Would you like cold-cereal or hot-cereal?" Gran Gran asked as I made myself into the kitchen. Hot cereal? I questioned in my head, why would anyone eat cereal hot? This place was getting weirder and weirder. "I've never had hot-cereal before," I replied.

She looked back, confused, as I felt inside and pulled a box of oatmeal with assorted flavors down from the cabinet. "Oh, you meant oatmeal," I said and chuckled, which she didn't find as humorous as I did.

For the next few weeks, Gran Gran would spend half the time correcting my speech and educating me on what she considered proper etiquette. There were no televisions in the house so I had to endure it all. She insisted I read or entertain myself in the huge backyard to pass the time. She took me to my first Book Fair out in Clayton. It was weird for me to see my classmates outside of school hours, as no Black kid ever stuck around because we couldn't miss our bus back to the city. I missed Mother and the girls so much and wondered how they were holding up in that rehabilitation castle. I'd never been out of their presence for more than a day and here it was going on four weeks. But I had my own room in a huge fancy house, all the food I could eat, and was chauffeured to and from school every day. However, I still would have preferred to be back out our meager home. Christmas had snuck up without much anticipation this year. I was stuck in Gran Gran's house and every day seemed like it ran together, there was no real sense of time. She woke me up early that morning and told me to go downstairs.

"Merry Christmas," she cheerily said, to which I groggily replied the same, wiping sleep from my eyes.

The living room floor was cluttered with neatly wrapped presents in colorful paper. I eagerly fell to my knees, ripping the colorful paper to shreds. In any other instance, I would have been mildly disappointed to have all these packages reveal shirts, sweaters, and pants as each box did here, one after the next. But I found meaningful appreciation in that moment of Gran Gran caring about my wellbeing, and taking Mother to get help. She wasn't my blood kin, and had only known my murdered Grandfather years ago, and still she had the patience to care. Christmas wasn't about the latest Sega games or new basketball shoes in that moment. After I finished unwrapping my gifts and cleaned up my mess, Gran Gran put on a perplexed face and asked, "Did you hear that? Out there by the side door, go have a look."

I didn't hear anything, but did as instructed. I walked past the long dining room table that could have seated fifteen people, to the wide glass patio doors showing the still dark and dank morning.

"I don't see anything," I said, turning to walk back.

"Go check again."

I wiped my eyes for a clearer look but still didn't see anything except trees blowing in the wind. I looked up to see silver wind chime tubes slightly swaying. "Maybe you heard this metal ornament thing?" I said.

"No, it wasn't that," Gran Gran said matter of factly. "Have a look one more time."

I was now a little annoyed, and I wondered what weird lesson she was trying to teach me. I stood at the patio window and looked all around for what she could've heard, then I lowered my eyes and saw a tall red mountain bike leaning on its kickstand right there on the back porch. I smiled a hard grin, now realizing she was hinting towards the brand new bike the whole time. I thanked her for all the gifts and was ecstatic to find out the best Christmas gift of the day was that I'd get to home that coming weekend.

CHAPTER 14

The only memory I had of Mother's stay at the Queen of Peace was a bronze colored medallion with the Serenity Prayer on it that she brought home. She said it was important that we remembered it and randomly tested us to say it aloud:

God, grant me the serenity to accept the things I cannot change,

Courage to change the things I can,

And wisdom to know the difference.

Unfortunately, addiction was much too powerful and the bronze medal wasn't strong enough to maintain Mother's sobriety. We moved a block over across Euclid Avenue onto Leduc Street, and the heartache of addiction got even worse. It was a more spacious duplex, and for the first time in my life, I had my very own room without the twins. However, the neighborhood wasn't better at all. In St. Louis, dynamics changed from block to block, and Leduc had a reputation for being the wildest in the area. Mother did a poor job of hiding her usage now, barricading herself behind the rickety wooden bathroom door to use.

I was a little older now nearing twelve and was growing into my manhood, so there were times when I would try to shoulder my way in the door, banging and kicking, trying to get in, tearful in the process, but I was still a child who couldn't compete with the power of an adult with a habit. I woefully accepted this fact, and the twins and I started to use the circumstances to our advantage.

They didn't yet understand the battle Mother was fighting, however, they did recognize her physical behavioral changes. When Mother was talking with cluttered speech and her hands and face moved freely on their own regard, what I knew of her being high, the girls said she was "happy." And whenever Mother was "happy," whatever appealing snack that most of the time was off limit to us, turned us into opportunists, and we seized the forbidden goodies for our own consumption. The expensive cookies she bought just for her and kept in her room, unopened ice cream, desserts before dinner ... it didn't matter, as she wasn't in her right mind to say no. We would wait and wait, and as soon as she showed symptoms of being under the influence, we'd pounce.

One day, I thought I'd put her vulnerability to the ultimate test, even though I fully expected her to come to her senses in the moment. For as long as I could remember I wanted a dog and was still holding out hope after so many failed dog hunts and Mother just flat out saying no, it was likely a lost cause. A friend of mine from over on Lotus had a dog who recently had a litter of puppies. We cared for the dogs every day from staggering balls of fur to being fully weaned from their mother and rambunctiously ready for new homes. I knew just the one I wanted: a fat little girl, sandy brown in color, with a black stripe going from her back to the tip of her tail. I had a name for her already. I would call her "Key," but I just knew Mother wouldn't let me bring her home. I peeked from the hallway through her bedroom door that was slightly ajar, studying her mannerisms and movements.

"Mother?" I said, peeking my head through door, trying to better gauge her current disposition.

"Here I ... I'll be out in a minute."

Hearing her response and seeing her twitching eyebrows, I knew I had to act fast. I then set my nerves aside and asked, "Well, Mikey's dog just had puppies and I was wondering if I can have one? Please. Pretty please?"

"Boy ... if you don't ... yes, yes ... I'll be out in a minute."

I accepted the parsed "yes" as an irrefutable approval and jetted out of the room. I ran full speed towards Mikey's house to pick up Key. The next day, I noticed Mother looking into the backyard through the screen door, fully sobered and wearing a serious face. I just knew I'd have to take Key back, and waited for the word. Key didn't help her case squatting in the middle of yard to take a shit with Mother watching.

"Um, clean that shit up now and then come get this money, you gotta go down to Northland Market and get some food for that thing. Call your Uncle Dan to see how many times a day he eats."

"It's a girl," I said with a wide sunny grin, acknowledging Mother's instruction and reading the friendly concession on her face, both of us well aware of the disjointed conversation the day before that brought a mess to her yard at that moment.

CHAPTER 15

I could smell the scent of fried chicken gizzards coming from the kitchen way out on the fronts steps were we sat. And apparently, the smell permeated the entire block, as a few neighborhood kids and thugs started making their way to our front lawn. The scene wasn't that unusual; Mother was a self-admitted friendly-bob who passed out food plates to almost anyone. She could have had a serious business had she not been so kind to hand out freebies mostly. My friend Eugene from across the street made his way over for his fixing I suspected, but I wasn't too thrilled; he was more of a friend by proximity as nobody really liked him much. He seemed to always be on a mission to overcompensate for his tight little curls and pretty boy looks, he'd much rather be seen as one of feared tough guys on the block. He poked and bullied whomever he could in an attempt to build a reputation. Besides regular roughhousing, we only came close to blows once, and it was Keisha who started it all.

One night, Eugene was putting on his usual tough guy act, and Keisha… having more confidence than

height herself, spoke up about how he was all talk.
Eugene's pride was too self-important, so he couldn't
dare handle slights from a pint-sized little girl. He
threatened to hit her with a metal dog chain he had
been holding if she'd dare say it again. Keisha wasted
no time pondering the threat and immediately told
him to do it. Eugene flung his arm sideways, like a
baseball pitcher, and launched the balled up metal
chain at her knees. Kya ran in the house, and like the
majority of any altercations I had, I was left to jump
in and defend my loudmouth sister.

I pushed Eugene, and we squared up to fight, circling
each other like old time boxers. Mother busted out
the front door, causing everyone to freeze and focus
on her energy. She came out in a threatening trot with
a leather belt flung over her shoulder, ready to swing.
To everyone's surprise, she was heading straight
towards me. My feet were glued to the pavement. I
was scared and confused as to why I was about to feel
her wrath, but luckily the twins screamed for her to
stop. Mother explained that it was about to be my ass
on the line if I hadn't defended my little sisters, to
which they quickly corrected her. Mother's fiery
entrance sort of diffused the whole situation, and no
one was in the mood to fight after that.

 A couple of the local dopeboys from up the block
made their way to our steps. Mother treated them no
differently than our friends, whom she would tease
and joke around with, and fed them like any hungry
mouth. I could see Eugene staring at the guy the
hood called Crater; he was only a couple years older
than us

but he ran with all the older guys, hustling and gangbanging. I could see the glimmer in Eugene's eyes as he studied in admiration the dress and swagger of ghetto opulence. His eyes followed them into the house, only then bringing his focus back to our routine kid things.

After a while, I was bored with front porch lounging and turned to Eugene. I said,

 "Let's go in the house and get on the game." He followed behind me as I walked toward Mother's room to ask if it was okay if I had company over. I could see Mother just entering her bedroom, with Crater following closely behind her, closing the door after they both entered. I paused dead in my tracks, shaken by the timing of everything. Eugene turned to me and screeched in an anxious whisper, "Yoooo, is Crater and your moms in there having sex?"

"No," I sternly replied in a flat tone, adding, "are you fucking crazy?" I said this while shifting my uneasiness towards him. I motioned him to my bedroom, and started the Sega, not entertaining his initial question and not wanting a reply to mine. I stared into space, making no mention of the awkward sight, all while we played the game that day, hoping it caused some distraction. The truth was I knew Mother was buying drugs, but knowing that didn't make it feel better to correct any wild assumptions. I was saddened and ashamed, and the fact that her

situation involved my peers made me feel like the
tiniest person on earth.

Only a fool would have believed that that awkward,
but sensitive, situation involving Mother would never
come up again from a low-minded jerk like Eugene.
And he brought it up the first chance he got. The
twins and I were out front deeply invested in a
shouting match with Eugene and his two sisters, who
stood in the street. It started over something petty,
more than likely Keisha and Eugene's clashing of
bravado, now corralling two families to stand their
ground and tongue jostle for upness. We traded
pathetically immature insults, one after another, then
Eugene pulled his trump card shouting, "That's why
yo momma on crack!"

I waited no time for the premeditated insult to
penetrate, and avengingly hollered back "And that's
why yo daddy uses heroin, bitch!" Both sides seemed
a bit stunned that each family had stooped so low to
be as hideously foul as possible, but we tried our best
not to let it show. I had no idea how I knew David's
father was a heroin addict. He lived in one of the few
homes in the whole neighborhood that had a father
figure in the home, and he also built Key a doghouse
by hand, just for me, after constructing one for
Eugene's new puppy. The ills that people suffered
behind closed doors wasn't much of a secret at all, I
just knew his dad was on drugs. But it made me
wonder, who all knew Mother struggled with crack

addiction? Mother was healthy, beautiful, and spirited, and wore no obvious suggestions of drug usage. We'd seen friends our age ripped from their homes due to so-called unfit living conditions, but Mother was functioning with a regular job and had us in school every day. None of that mattered as we kids stood right here in the streets, flinging venomous insults about demons our parents were battling.

CHAPTER 16

I had to find escapes from the draining and dismal sadness that home life could be at times. School was my only true getaway, miles away from the violence of the connected blocks I walked, and it gave me a focus from worrying about the wellbeing of Mother. Camping, skiing trips, and visiting wolf sanctuaries were all welcome school activities and field trips that brought me into a world of enthusiastic hope and vivid dreams that I never imagined existed. These things may have been normal for most kids at my school, but it was my refuge.

Walking in the house one day after school, the peculiar burning aroma was lingering in the air and I knew Mother was high before I briefly greeted her. I didn't pay much mind to it as my stomach spoke its language of hunger, which led me to the kitchen. Still unwinding from the long school day, I went to my bedroom, tossing my bulky backpack to the floor. I immediately noticed my Sega game system was missing from the television stand. Doing a double take, I squinted around and assured myself it was certainly not there. I feverishly sprinted to Mother's room and shouted, "We've been robbed! My Sega is gone!"

"No . . . what?" Mother replied.

"Yeah, it's gone."

"Well go check again."

I went back to the room, looking under every corner and space I could find. "Why would somebody take my stuff? What kind of asshole would break-in and steal from a poor kid?" I said. "Fuck!"

The emotional violation I felt in that moment was immensely sickening. We didn't have a whole lot of value, and this system was one of the few things I cherished, one of the few places I could escape to at home and break from all my worries. I went back to report no finding to Mother. I explained to her that my television and everything was just how I left it, all but the Sega. I pestered her with questions about how long she'd been home, and who'd been there, if the doors were locked, did the landlord stop over, all trying to piece together how this culprit made off with my gaming system.

Mother only gave me half thoughts and no clarity at all. I was growing more and more frustrated.

"Go check outside . . . check the dumpster," Mother blurted.

Already dejected, I didn't put much thought in the suggestion as I still held out hope that it would pop up somewhere. I peered out at the mostly empty block, with the streetlights overhead still dim, as evening had only just begun. My walk slowed to a slothful pace. I could see the large brown dumpster ahead but didn't understand what I was going to look for. I started to drag my feet, and with each soft step, it became clearer what happened to my belongings. For all the wrenching heartache we dredged through over these soiled years, Mother had never once let her habit conflict with her children in such a way. The deep sorrow still weighed me down as I got only inches from the dumpster. I went through the motions of lifting the lid and checking behind it, knowing there was nothing but the intended garbage there. I just couldn't confront Mother; the pity I felt for her made the stupid game seem meaningless. Whatever little hope I had for her recovery paled in comparison to the power this drug had on her now; she was in its clutches.

CHAPTER 17

The hard aluminum mesh of the front screen door had a stench of saliva, dust, and probably whatever bothersome insects that got caught in its web. . My face pressed up against the wiry diamond shapes, I was watching an argument ensue between Crater's people from up the block and the Thompson family, who stayed right at the house on the corner of Euclid Avenue and Leduc Street.

More and more people entered, bickering, coming from different directions. I noticed one youngster walking steadily past the house with his arm stiffened at his sides like a Nutcracker soldier holding a frosty silver pistol. One of the Thompsons countered by grabbing a long rifle from the house and concealing it under his shirt. The poorly hidden weapons quieted the bickering and turned the confrontation into harsh promises from both sides that they'd return later; broad daylight was hardly a time for such theatrics.

I pulled my smushed face from the screen, leaving its pattern in my skin and went to tell Mother of the happenings outside, but she showed little interest. She was in an even-keeled demeanor, but something was cryptic about her mood that I couldn't put a finger on. This only got worse a little later that evening when Mother called to us. She handed each of us a black trash bag and said, "I want y'all to fill these bags up with as many of your clothes you can fit in there. We're going to the laundromat."

The orders were barked with a serious tone and an unsmiling face, so the twins and I knew not to ask any questions right then. She yelled from her room for us to hurry up because a taxi was on its way. We dragged our bags to the front, and I saw Mother's glossy eyes and steely face had remained unchanged. I couldn't gauge where this was coming from because we hadn't been to a laundromat in years, and there was a perfectly good washing machine in the basement.

Before I could try to soften her up or further investigate, the taxicab was honking the horn outside. We stuffed our filled bags in the trunk with a little help from the driver, who politely asked Mother where we were headed.

"To the Greyhound Station, Cass Avenue," Mother said to the taxi driver as the cab pulled off.

"Greyhound Station?" I questioned. I looked at Mother and could tell she had been crying. Her face was less stiff now and she shifted to the attention of us three children.

"Where are we going?" Kya asked Mother.

"I don't know yet."

"We're not going to the laundromat?"

"No," Mother answered, sniveling and fighting back a teary flow.

The ceilings of the Greyhound bus station were high enough to park a bus right there inside. I stared at the lights of the rectangle board with endless cities and times listed on it, and listened to huge buses all lined up perfectly behind us, with people shouting out things and hustling this way and that way. It was a wonder how anyone knew where they were going with such frenzied commotion going on.

Mother finally got to the ticket counter after an exhausting wait. I could overhear her discussing Ohio with the ticket agent. The only time I'd heard of Ohio was from our cousins who stayed around the corner on Hammett Place, as their momma moved there about a year ago with all five kids in tow. Everything seemed surreal.

Why were we here in this loud and busy bus station, at a ticket counter, and discussing Ohio? It didn't make sense; I wanted to go home. I could see the man at the ticket counter shaking his head at Mother and saying, ". . . nothing until tomorrow at the earliest."

Mother looked around at the roaring buses behind us as they waited to depart.

"What's the next bus leaving?" she asked the man.

The man paused before speaking, looking down at his screen. "We have a . . . Columbia. Columbia, Missouri leaving in thirty minutes."

"You know anything about Columbia?"

"Uh no, sorry I don't," the man replied, scrunching his face in a puzzled manner, looking down at our little black faces and hands holding the bags of clothes.

"I'll take four tickets," Mother said.

The bus was dark and crowded.   We climbed into our cramped seats that rumbled with the noisy engine. Every seat was filled with all people that had a destination in mind that evening. I was sure we were the only ones who didn't know what awaited us. We were simply following, or trusting, Mother, to wherever that led us.

  The bus took off, and the realization of what was happening set in for the twins, who started to sob and whine. They badgered Mother with question after question. "But what about school tomorrow? And all our stuff? How will anybody know where we are? We don't know anybody there. You're leaving your brand new furniture, Mother? When are we coming back? . . . Where will we sleep?"

"We're going to sleep in a box, outside in an alley!" I interrupted sourly, cutting off the barrage of questioning, as being mean-spirited and obnoxious were the only feelings I could conjure up at the time before Mother warned me to stop. The most appropriate time to be somber was right then, leaving everything we knew, everything we owned, everything we loved while heading to nowhere. But feeling anything else felt useless right then. I just rode along, until after a couple hours with one stop, we finally reached the Greyhound Bus Station in Columbia, MO. It was a pitifully modest building, and fairly empty, nothing like the station we left back in St. Louis. It was eerily quiet with no workers at all, only a couple passengers besides us.

After a while, we were the only ones there, with Keisha and Kya asleep on benches and Mother fumbling through yellow pages at a payphone as I watched on. We were alone, in the middle of a strange town we'd never heard of, and unable to turn back.

CHAPTER 18

We had been in the Women's Shelter (The Shelter as we called it) for a month. We would be held up uproariously by watching the local news like it was a Thursday night sitcom. I would anticipate goofy news stories like A Cat Got Saved from a Tree, or Old Lady Crosses Road. It should have been refreshing to hear feel good stories on TV, but we were so jaded by salaciousness and crime coverage that this broadcast seemed like a parody.

The Shelter was a welcome place, given the circumstances that we warmed to instantaneously. It still seemed like just yesterday we were at the dinghy Greyhound Station all by ourselves with nowhere to go. I don't recall the trip, but somehow we ended up at the Salvation Army that day; they didn't even have beds for us and had to pull out low-lying cots to sleep on. Mother had a couple of meetings with the counselor there, and before we got to learn anyone's name, we were out and ended up here.

The Shelter was an adult women's residential center that already had about ten woman living there. The women were there from all corners of the state, for everything from substance abuse treatment to escaping being killed by their husbands and boyfriends. For that reason, there was a building policy that we couldn't disclose our location to anyone, as the last thing anyone wanted was some crazed lunatic finding his woman who had run away for a new chance at life.

The staff immediately took a liking to our family and adored us all. It may have been because we were a lot less obnoxious than some of the wild little kids already there who were ripping through the hallways. It didn't take long to start to shake off the joyless stench we carried here with our single trash bags. We had nothing but each other, so every new experience in this stale little town brought life to our being. There were amusing hiccups as we adjusted to our new lives; finding black churches and barbershops was the first hurdle.

In the first barbershop Mother took me to, we were greeted by an old white man. Mother asked him if he could cut a little black boy's hair. He said yes, we took him for his word until he pulled out scissors and snipped and chopped away, doing absolutely nothing for my thick nappy hair. We left before he tried his hot towel thingy.

Mother had her own inglorious welcome as she nearly had a panic attack at the sight of a Deer Crossing sign while visiting my new school for the first time. I guess she assumed it to mean wild deer were prowling nearby and would launch a sudden pouncing attack at a moment's notice.

We would remain at The Shelter up into Christmas time. By then Mother had started working and seemed to be not only healthy and cheerful, but settled. Everything we left behind didn't seem to hold any real value now, except for Key, who I reminded Mother we had left behind in the backyard. She claimed that Ms. Thompson had gone over and picked her up and was raising her. I didn't know if I believed that but I convinced myself Key was all right.

Christmas morning at The Shelter was one I'd remember for a long while. The counselors there had asked all the children what they'd like for Christmas, and I told them I'd like a Sega, but I didn't go into details of how mine was lost. They said that was a little out of their price range, which I accepted. Their idea was to give the children more generic things, such as footballs and clothes, which they could hand out to all the kids without much thought. All the kids in the center ran down to the tall, bright, Christmas tree, digging through boxes, looking for our names. I found two similar, large, boxes with my name on them in different wrappings. I frantically ripped through the thin paper of the first one, unable to limit my excitement at uncovering a brand new Sega. The second box was tagged 'From Mother,' and I ripped the paper just as fast as the first and this too was a brand new Sega!

CHAPTER 19

We grew into our newly adopted little college town figuratively and literally, receiving graduation credits in place of gold stars in school. We lived in a modest but comfortable home, which was a longshot from when we first left The Shelter. Our first place was a housing project apartment, with only one piece of furniture we picked up from the thrift store, which was an unattractive pink cubicle made as a desk, chair, or whatever we found use for it until we finally got some actual furniture.

Mother seemed to find herself there. She had lived a life five times over while dealing with the ills of the grimiest St. Louis had to offer, and the slow pace and quiet of Columbia was perfect for her at this stage of her life. She found a church home she was comfortable with and developed a meaningful relationship with God. I still had reservations about her sobriety and that fear of what it was like when drugs seized her body, and I knew relapse was more common than soberness. I came home from school every day and routinely took a studied look at her, just as I did as a young kid, expecting her to be "happy".... under the influence as the twins called. One day after school, I came upstairs to her room and took a quick glance around. She called me back in the room before I could step away.

"You don't have to check on me anymore," she said in the purest tone I'd ever heard from her. With that simple statement, we both understood that we both were fully aware of the worries of this routine over all these years, and that this was something we'd never have to agonize over again. I don't know what to owe it to, whether it be faith or simply being tired, but Mother reminded me later that her addiction was a never ending battle and I was thankful she was a courageous fighter. Her spirit never left her, and now when she talked and talked to whatever stranger happened to get caught in her web, she just had to add her testimony about her battles to overcome addiction. My annoyance and embarrassment was still there but I was undoubtedly proud. I never really questioned if the long and grueling road to get to this point had to be traveled as such. I accepted the fact that our tumultuous journey could only be endured by us and found peace and purpose in making it through.

CHAPTER 20

Mother's new fight of raising teenagers alone may have been her most taxing yet, how she navigated the perils of St. Louis with us was admirable. We followed in line, confronting fear head-on, mostly due to our trust and love for her. But for a teenager's independence, or at least the perception of it, this was the finish line for a marathon of a fatiguing adolescence. Every bit of advice or instruction from adults was recognized as an interrogation, so adherence gave a sense of manipulative vulnerability and unwanted exposure. Mother wasn't bashful about reminding us that she was doing it on her own. I sparingly spoke to Big Quinn, and had lowered expectations of hearing from him many years ago. On the other hand, Mother kept in touch with him quite often but mainly to check on his well-being. She mentioned to me that he had been struggling with his own heroin addiction for years. The only knowledge I had of this drug was when, on a visit back to St. Louis once, we heard Eugene's dad had lost his battle with the drug and was found dead from an overdose in his bathroom. I couldn't imagine how Eugene must have felt. Mother insisted that our father was doing fine, and didn't put any worry on us.

Keisha's teenage height had now finally caught up to the bluster she exuded as an overconfident kid. With that, came school fight after school fight, and disciplinary action wasn't much of a deterrent. We had grown out of belt whoopings, and Mother was improbably tasked with wrangling a formidable bull without the use of leather straps.

There was one girl named Tishawna that Keisha spoke of nearly every day after school. It was mostly normal girly bickering but I could feel the atmospheric tension rise as each day passed. Keisha and her classmates mockingly referred to the girl as "Bear" when they spoke amongst themselves; this was due to her unmissable hulking size. Mother tried her best to quell any conflicts by talking sense into Keisha, and even threatening her whenever Bear came up, but whether it was a test of wills or an insensible appetite to put her hands to the test, a fight was inevitable.

After Mother got the call at home about the fight, which included desk and chairs flying across the room, she made it a point to make frequent visits to the school, if not for anything else, but to have her agitating presence felt. She even went out of her way one time to awkwardly ask a random student, "Where is Bear?" To which the red-faced little girl sheepishly replied, "You mean Tishawna?" giggling at the slip. Mother was a people person, and she just wanted to talk and throw in one of her testimonies, she now acted as the ultimate intermediator.

For the twins to act alike in so many ways, besides their skin tone, the main distinguishing feature between them was that Kya was always accused of acting grown. Being born only two minutes earlier than Keisha, one would think that measly minute of head start wouldn't be a catapult for adulthood, but it was. As early as Kya knew cuss words were for adults, she liberally flung them at us when provoked … out of earshot of Mother. She now acted out her grownness in sexual precocity. Mother once called me, in tears, and I immediately figured someone had died because her voice was barely audible.

"Kya is pregnant," she said, pushing out her words. We all felt an overwhelming sense of hurt and disappointment. I don't think anyone was truly aware of the source of hurt, besides the obvious negatives of being pregnant while still in high school, and not being in a position to support a child.

I took my unsettled frustrations out on Mother, misguidedly blaming her for the entire situation. We spoke about how to handle it ad nauseam, with Mother even calling a family meeting with the boy in attendance. She ultimately decided to abort the pregnancy. A decision Mother stated was by all accounts hers, and which she later deeply regretted.

One early Saturday morning, I was awakened by rude and authoritative knocking at the front door that for some reason no one else in the house took liberty to answer. My annoyance skyrocketed when Mother walked past the front door, opened my bedroom door, and instructed me to go see who it was. I made my way to the door after yelling muffled expletives into the thick of my pillow. I swung open the door to surprisingly see an Asian man and a Black man standing upright and nobly in full Army fatigues and boots. I just knew this was Mother's doing, and the soldiers got a good chuckle out of the fact that I had no idea they were coming. This wasn't the first of these weirdly sly schemes Mother had pulled off for me.

One summer she had the bright idea to sign me up for Junior Police Academy. After the third painstakingly dull meeting, I decided to skip the rest of the classes and told Mother that I graduated. Then there was the time she cussed me out after leaving a career counselor she forced me to meet with, telling me to never again tell someone I wanted to be a professional sports player. I thought I was being honest when asked to pick my absolute dream job, but given that I hadn't played organized football since giving the middle finger to Matthew Dickey's, she was probably right. Even though she was hilariously random in her efforts, I knew exactly what Mother was trying to do. Long before I had any idea what it meant, and my only interest was in cartoons, she preached about the importance of not becoming another Black male statistic.

We watched as violence and drugs wrecked our neighborhoods and sucked the blood out of Black boys, and how the system then chewed them up and fed on their soulless bodies. She feared I would share the same fate with so few positive male influences in my life. She now openly congratulated me on not being a statistic, but was afraid that if I didn't have defined goals following high school graduation, then I could easily fall into the trappings of our society.

CHAPTER 21

Mother was serenely enjoying her time having an empty nest, and she was not the least bit bashful about telling us to keep our asses away. The twins had their own respective houses not too far from Mother, and I had my own back in St. Louis all having graduated high school by now. She welcomed the simple life, and that it was, sharing her time between a regular routine of church, work, and her male friend. She also finally found a way to reap the most benefit from her years of sharing impromptu testimonies to any stranger that had ears, as she now headed a Prison Ministry, sharing the Gospel to inmates and youth offenders.

Mother was happy, and had found triumphant peace and the sense of resolve she had gambled on years ago at that Greyhound ticket counter. She even had her gold tooth pulled, which made her feel liberated and more in harmony with her present self. There were additions to the family too, as fate saw Keisha and Kya get pregnant at the same time and deliver a girl, then a boy within weeks of each other. Mother adored her grandchildren, taking them on library trips and smothering them with affection before the twins got too comfortable with their alone time.

Things took a sudden drastic change in the early part of February. Mother had complained of pressure on her abdomen causing some discomfort for a while, and after finally visiting a doctor, she was scheduled for a common, low-risk, gallbladder removal surgery. She called me from the hospital that day.

"Quinn . . . I need you to listen. I can't call everyone so I need you to pass this information on to everybody in St. Louis for me."

"Okay, what's going on?" I interrupted.

Mother replied firm but calmly, "They did a biopsy and found cancer in my gallbladder, it hasn't spread to my lymph nodes though."

"Whaaat, cancer? I gasped in a confused manner, adding, "What does this mean? I don't understand. Are you okay? Who's there with you?"

"I'm fine," Mother said, still calm. "That's all I know right now, they have to do some additional testing but I'm okay. TT Darcy is on the way."

I made the calls Mother requested as best I could, but I could only relay the message in a childlike tone, there was no fluidity or real coherence of what I was repeating. I could only hear the word, cancer, in my head, repeating over and over again. I was filled with vague but heavy fear.

Over the next couple of weeks after the diagnosis, I would do my own tireless research for better understanding, but nothing I read made me feel more hopeful. Cancer was equal to death, but with the death of a Grandmother and Aunts over the years, it still was tied to older age, one of those things that just happened at that stage of your life. But Mother was only 47, barely a grandmother and she kept a young glowing spirit, so it didn't make sense. Her unyielding positivity and calmness were the only things that kept everyone's head on straight. It was infectious and you couldn't help but become part of the boundless optimism, no matter how unjustifiable it may have really been. For her, the affliction only strengthened her faith in the Lord as she accepted sickness as part of his righteousness and was thankful to be where she stood in her faith at the time of the diagnosis. She would say she couldn't fathom such news coming at a different time in her life.

Further tests categorized the cancer at stage IV, and Mother quickly began radiation treatments, to be followed by chemotherapy. We all accompanied her for a hospital visit in March. There were at least fifteen of us … family and a couple of close friends. I counted them all crammed in the single patient room as I walked in. Surely, we did not care about capacity or any restrictive rules at that moment. We all engaged in cheery conversation and recounted silly happenings going on in our lives, surrounding Mother's bedside and exchanging laughs, her wit never waning. I stepped back and took a moment to observe her lying under bleached white sheets on the high bed. She sounded somewhat groggy and even appeared a bit tired, but her face was still full and bright.

Mother could sense my uneasiness, and she called me over next to the bed, gently grabbing my fingers and assuring me she was okay. I forced a lopsided and insincere smirk, and nodded to let her know I heard her before fading behind everyone's shoulders again. The jovial laughs started to sound like hollow words after a while, just noises bouncing off the simple plain walls of the room.

Am I the only one who understands the gravity of the situation? I thought. I could feel my body slowly tensing up. Mother shouldn't be here, I shouldn't be here, no one should, and especially not in this predicament, I thought. I tried to tiptoe towards the door, then I heard Mother call out to me, "Where's Quinn?"

"Your Mother wants you," someone said behind me, unaware of me stepping aside in the midst of all the banter. I ignored the calls, pushing through the wide door. I immediately burst into despairing and steady tears that had been pent up the entire time I was in the room. The thought of Mother not being here with us was unfathomable; her journey was nowhere near its ending, not like this. I collected myself and came back into Mother's comforting hand, "What's wrong?" she asked.

"I just don't wanna lose you."

CHAPTER 22

Mother's patience was short, and she was considerably grumpier, according to a heads up from the family, who knew I was coming down from St. Louis for the weekend. I was interested to see what all the fuss was about. I arrived at the house to find just her and my ten-year-old cousin Jasmine there.

"So you dun ran everybody off huh?" I said with a teasing grin to mother.

She responded with a hmph sound under her breath before saying, "You see who's here don't you?" implying that someone should have been. My aunt, her daughter Jackie, and the twins had been in a rotation, keeping eyes on Mother and tending to her needs. I guess I was the assumed de facto next man up, coming in town for the weekend.

"Yeah, where is TT or the girls at?"

"Your TT is still a little sister. After all these years too. And let me show you this shit the girls brought over. I asked them to bring me some chicken."

Mother stopped talking for a second and pulled a box of frozen wings picked up from the nearby grocery store. "What am I supposed to do with this shit?" she said, obviously irritated. I laughed hysterically, causing Mother to crack a smile in the middle of her rant.

"And Jasmine just been here talking my head off," she added, with both of us now openly laughing and finding amusement in the vexed state of affairs. Jasmine and I entertained ourselves with music and board games while Mother got some rest. We would stay tightly glued by Mother's side for the next few days, taking care of hers needs between the frequent naps. It was apparent now that Mother wasn't just being ornery to be ornery. She was frustrated that her body was failing her and she couldn't get things done as she normally would on her own.

Sitting there those hours I thought about how, for so many years, she was the unquestioned caregiver for everyone. As far back as Bacon Street, and in every single home we lived in after that, Mother always had some child; a cousin or a family friend she would take on to care for. Whether their momma was incarcerated or strung out on drugs, even while Mother had her own struggles, she still had the wherewithal to care for someone else.

After Grandmamma White died, Mother became the unofficial Big Momma of the family; it was meant to be and seemed to just fall into place. Even after we made the impulsive move to this little town no one

had ever heard of, TT Darcy and her children
followed, then Uncle Dan, Uncle Elmer and more
family members followed Mother here. She had been
a mother to so many for years, giving herself
tirelessly, now she barely had energy to stay awake.
This would be the last time I physically recognized
the Mother that raised and loved me. The radiation
and chemotherapy had failed; the cancer resisted, and
was slowly and painfully eating away at her body.

When the news came that she was determined to be
terminally ill, and was referred to at-home hospice
care, it did little to change my level of sorrow. From
that very first call back in February I'd been mentally
preparing myself for the death of my mother. In early
July, the sixth month since that call, TT Darcy called
to tell me to come down as they didn't expect Mother
to last through the weekend.

CHAPTER 23

Mother lay in her own bed, on her back, skin and bones from the cruel and incurable cancer. Her eyes stared wide, off towards the ceilings, and had no life about them, never moving as I walked to her bedside.

"You can talk to her, she can still hear you," TT Darcy said as she held a straw to Mother's lips.

Mother slightly lifted her head towards the straw, appearing to use every ounce of energy she had left in her debilitated body. "Yeah, we've been talking to her," Kya added.

I couldn't bring myself to speak. I placed my hand on her arm, angled at her side with one of her fists tightly clenching a small wooden cross. I just sat. Visitors came by every hour, bearing flowers and balloons, and said their well wishes. I appreciated the gestures but asked TT Darcy if she could stop any more guest from coming up. Mother's condition was worsening as the hours passed; her eyes were still lifeless and her breaths were short, shallow gasps. Her mouth stayed slightly open and I could hear fight for each breath. TT Darcy and I stayed with Mother as everyone else went home to get some sleep and planned to meet back in the morning. I sat downstairs, unable to sleep after seeing my Mother that way, fighting for every breath. Her body looked soulless, and I just wanted her pain to end. She had once described the pain as having a thousand needles pressing against her stomach; that was no way to live.

"Quinn, are you awake?" TT Darcy said, tiptoeing down the steps early that morning while it was still fairly dark outside.

"Yes, I'm up."

"Okay, I think it's time," she said.

I hurriedly hopped up, following her to the bedroom. Upon entering, I reached for Mother's arm, and was taken aback by the iced coldness I felt. Why is it so cold in here? I thought. I looked up to see the ceiling fan was on, and stood up, reaching toward the pull chain to try to make it warmer for Mother, but before I could reach the wooden knob on the end, I froze as the realization came to me. She was gone.

It felt like Mother had been preparing us for her untimely absence our entire lives, but she was such a massive and gracious presence that the thought never crossed anyone's mind before those short six months. Now we were motherless, like children lost in an amusement park. There was a sweeping sense of fear; there were good and bad people around, things to charm our minds, even familiar sights, but nothing felt safe to trust without her. A terrifying sense of desperation and recklessness swelled in me as more time passed; there was no one on earth to answer to and no one to pray for me like Mother did. I could only cling to the moral lessons I gathered from her over the years in hopes to navigate this wicked world. All my grandparents had long been dead so their unerring wisdom faded and could provide no comfort now. I dredged forward, nearly emotionless, almost robotic, just to function properly.

CHAPTER 24

I found some small but warm solace in the fact that we still had our father. There had been years of laborious emotional building to completely cover the void he left in being mostly absent, so much so that it felt uncomfortable to expect anything of him at this point. There was no hate or resentment on my part, so when I got the call that he needed a place to stay, I accepted him without question. My father popping up so sudden should have been met with thorough interrogation from me, a search for some satisfactory answers on why he should have had more of a presence but I didn't have it in me. I needed him now since Mother's passing, and I was there for him as he stated he needed me currently. That did, however, put in perspective that he still didn't appear to be in a position to be the father we may have needed at the moment. He'd always been going through many revolving doors, not getting too comfortable on any particular couch. He brought only a few bags to my house, supporting his assurance that he just needed my help for about a week. He still told the same old stories, with vigor and enthusiasm, as if it were the first time I'd heard them. I wasn't sure if I'd remembered it as it happened as a child or just remembered it from one of his stories, but either way, his confidence was amusing, and the retellings never got boring.

What I never forgot though, was the putrid smell of his feet, as he quickly made himself comfortable by kicking off his shoes. The smell of hot, stewed, sweaty feet poisoned the air. His shoes had to be set on the patio, and that was pretty much the only rule I had to establish, otherwise an adequate breath couldn't be had in that hazardous mist.

One week of stay turned into weeks, then months. I had been holding off saying anything, but eventually I had to set an ultimatum for him to leave, otherwise he'd never have an incentive to find a place of his own. Even in leaving, we both were proud of the first real semblance of a father/son relationship being established. We were closer than we'd ever been, and every interaction, no matter how minute, had meaning, due to the many empty years that had to be made up.

He eagerly invited me over to his modest apartment every chance he got, proudly talking about the plans he had to fix up the place. Here I was in my mid-twenties celebrating Father's Day with him for the first time. My love for him could never be measured for what he did, because even though I was in the position of helping, more so than he was, it now had a presence that was invaluable. Keisha and Kya needed a little extra convincing from me to warm up to him, but they eventually came around. Ironically, the loss of Mother did the opposite of strengthening the need for another parent. Her loss made it nearly impossible for anyone to come in and try to fill her shoes, or even act in her manner. However, we all had to accept that there were other roles people could play in our lives without comparison.

CHAPTER 25

The functions that came with adulthood like daily work and relationships was nothing more than a tool to keep my mind from being fixed on losing Mother. I found a steady girlfriend; Carmen, but lacked the emotional responsibility to put forward the best me, and struggled having to add her shortcomings on to my woes. My optimism about life took a spirited boost after finding out Carmen was expecting a boy. A joy bubbled in my soul that I'd never experienced before. I was unaware just how mechanical I'd been in my mournful state. Now I wasn't consumed with the past feelings of bliss and innocence of my child-self to comfort my adult heartache. I had unfiltered hope for a bright and prosperous future for my unborn son. My family was equally excited for an extension of us, especially from lonesome me. My son's lively kicks from the warmth of his mom's belly did more to soothe my spirit than he'd ever know.

An early Saturday phone call woke me from my slumber on a cool but still pleasant October morning. I ignored it, hoping to steal an extra few minutes of sleep, but the phone rang again less than a minute later. I saw it was Keisha and picked up. "Quinn . . ." she shrieked in a harsh tone, "Daddy's dead."

"What?" I replied, hopping upward to the edge of the bed.

"I just got the call. They found him on his living room floor ... dead," Keisha said with her voice trembling in between crying.

"I gotta go, I'm heading over there now."

"Okay."

I hadn't fully processed the phone conversation I'd just had, because I drove teary-eyed towards my father's house with the intent of saving his life ... as if I had not just received word that he was gone. By the time I got there, a couple of my younger cousins greeted me and let me know his body had already been taken away. I entered the apartment and stood there alone in disbelief, thinking there was no way this was real. Whatever was left of my heart was broken again.

Three short years after losing our mother, we would have to put together plans to bury our father. Unlike Mother's death, there was no time to mentally prepare for this loss, for all we knew he had been completely healthy. The autopsy report came back a few weeks later, determining the cause of death was due to fentanyl intoxication from laced heroin.

After confirmation of the cause of death, it was hard not to look back at some possible warning signs or opportunities where I might have helped. But to be struck with dreadful lightning twice in such short time, left little room for reasoning; death was excessively cruel and unjust. You have no choice but to accept it as it knocks. I still asked God why he'd deal us such a cruel hand. Our despair was part of our being, engraved in our minds and flowing through our bodies like a slow but wretched poison. From my mother's childhood, which was robbed of the angelic purity that most kids share, the unknowing of an evil world inviting itself to your doorstep, life became a guide on survivorship. It was only natural that her seeds would inherit the ability to endure and master, smiling through anguish. Now we had to teach ourselves to live outside of our imaginations, to learn that life's desires cannot only be molded from rain-soaked clay but could grow and break the surface of earth's hardened core with sincere invitation from the rising sun and light winds, with watchful care there was already an urge to kiss the skies. Two days after my father's passing, my son was born—

ABOUT THE AUTHOR

Warren Armour was born and raised in St. Louis, Missouri. He is a graduate from Lindenwood University in St. Charles, Missouri. He dreams to one day live far out in the country and pass time by watching classic films, sports, and writing fiction novels. WHEN CLOUDS TAKE FORM is his debut novel.